THE BEDSIDE COMPANION
TO CRIME

THE BEDSIDE COMPANION TO CRIME

H.R.F. Keating

THE MYSTERIOUS PRESS
New York London Tokyo Sweden Milan

First published in Great Britain by
Michael O'Mara Books Ltd
9 Lion Yard, Tremadoc Road, London SW4

First Mysterious Press Printing: October 1989
THE MYSTERIOUS PRESS
129 West 56th Street
New York
NY 10019

10 9 8 7 6 5 4 3 2 1

ISBN 0-89296-416-2

LC 89-43167

Editors: Anne Forsyth and E.A. Prost
Design: Mick Keates

Typeset by Florencetype Ltd, Kewstoke, Avon
Printed and bound in Great Britain by
Butler and Tanner Ltd, Frome, Somerset

ACKNOWLEDGEMENTS

'Detective Story' from *Collected Poems* by W.H. Auden. By kind permission of
Faber and Faber and Random House, New York.

'Don't Guess Let Me Tell You' from *I Wouldn't Have Missed It* by Ogden
Nash. By kind permission of André Deutsch Ltd and Curtis Brown Group
Ltd.

'Denouement' by Reginald Hill. By kind permission of the author.

'The Guilty Party' by Julian Symons. By kind permission of Curtis Brown
Group Ltd.

'Send for Lord Timothy' by John Heath Stubbs. By kind permission of David
Higham Associates Ltd.

'The Owl Writes a Detective Story' from *Young Pobbles Guide to His Toes* by
Gavin Ewart. By kind permission of Century Hutchinson Publishing
Group Ltd.

'A Hell of a Writer' by Roger Woddis. By kind permission of Radio Times.

CONTENTS

A WORD BEFORE YOU
NOD OFF 7

10 LITTLE – WELL, TEN
LITTLE WHATS? 13

9 SLY GLANCES

Atlantic Crossings 18
Is They Is, Or Are They Ain't? 23
Errors and Omissions 27
Wrong Again 33
The Duller the Better 34
Who Killed Round Robin? 37
Scribble, Scribble, Mr Gribble 43
The Final Accolade 48
Never Mind the Great
Detectives . . . 49
   1. Fantomas 49
   2. Flambeau 49
   3. Fosco, Count 50
   4. Godahl, the Infallible 51
   5. Gurman, Caspar 51
   6. Lone Wolf, The 52
   7. Lovejoy 52
   8. Lugg, Magersfontein 53
   9. Lupin, Arsene 53
   10. Manchu, Dr Fu 54
   11. Mannering, John, also
      known as The Baron 55
   12. Mason, Randolph 55
   13. Moriarty, Professor James 56
   14. Peterson, Carl 56
   15. Raffles, A.J. 57
   16. Ripley, Tom 58
   17. Simpson, Arthur Abdel 58
   18. Teatime, Miss Lucilla 59
   19. Templar, Simon, otherwise
      the Saint 59
   20. Velvet, Nick 60

8 KINDS OF CRIMINOSITY

Hermetically Sealed 61
Schools for Skulduggery 66
Putting on the Mockers 71
Presence of Body 76
Brown Studies 82
Hissing Mysteries 88
Dead Funny 94
Breakfast, Lunch and Tea 101

7 SONGSTERS SINGING
or The Oxblood Book of
Detectival Verse 107

6 BEGINNINGS

Agatha Christie 118
Simenon 123
Michael Innes 128
Raymond Chandler 131
Ross Macdonald 136

5 FAVOURITES

The Moonstone 141
The Hound of the Baskervilles 144
The Maltese Falcon 149
The Talented Mr Ripley 153
A Taste for Death 156

4 GOOD OLD BOYS

R. Austin Freeman 160
Melville Davisson Post 163
Edgar Wallace 165
Jacques Futrelle 168

3 GOOD OLD GIRLS

Mary Roberts Rinehart 170
Gladys Mitchell 173
Margery Allingham 176

2 INTO ONE

Ellery Queen – Fred Dannay
and Manfred Lee 179
Emma Lathen – Jane Latris
and Martha Henissart 183

1 FEARFUL YELLOW

John D. MacDonald's
Obsession 185

AND THEN THERE
WERE NONE

The Christie Classic
Dismembered 187

INDEX 190

ILLUSTRATION SOURCES 192

Harry Clarke's illustration to 'The Murders in the Rue Morgue' which provides a
clue to the real killer for those who don't know the story.

A WORD
BEFORE YOU NOD OFF

Why do we read crime stories? Short answer: for fun. And, indeed, there is plenty of fun, of simple enjoyment, to be found in mystery fiction. I have long maintained, in fact, that it is the entertainment factor that differentiates crime fiction from novels that have a crime or a murder or a whole string of murders in them but are not crime fiction. The pure novelists write in order to tell us dumb readers something, and sometimes it's convenient for them to do so by means of a story or a situation that encompasses murder. Whereas a crime novelist writes first simply to hold the reader, to entertain the reader.

Crime writers, of course, may have something they want to tell readers, too. But, while they keep to the crime formula (which may be as complex as the formula for, say, LSD) they pause from time to time and ask themselves what their readers will be feeling. And if it's boredom, or the shadow of boredom, they do what Raymond Chandler said he did when he got into a jam, 'have a man come in the door with a gun'.

In the course of entertaining in this way in all the years since there has been mystery fiction, say from the first publication in 1841 of Edgar Allan Poe's story 'The Murders in the Rue Morgue' (and Poe had something to say in that, intriguing though the tale is) crime writers have produced an immense mound of fun facts. Fun facts, I call them for want of a better description. But by them I mean all the oddities and interesting bitzer that have slipped into the pages and, indeed, exuded from the lives.

So for this bedside companion (you can read it elsewhere, really) I have garnered as many of these fun facts as I could find or remember and arranged them in neat piles, with little flags on top like the ones on sandwiches at big tea parties to give a hint of what's inside.

But perhaps before tucking in it might be an idea to be reminded about indigestion. Not everybody reacts happily to cucumber, or crime. The art I love has as many detractors as *aficionados*. Most of the rude things that have been said about it over the years I have contrived totally to forget. But some of them linger all right.

There's a verse from *Punch*, which I can't say I have recalled with bitterness ever since 1925 as I wasn't born till a year later. But I have had it in the back of my mind, irritating as a fragment of gristle at the back of the teeth, ever since I first came across it.

> Detectives incredibly stupid
> And villains unspeakably vile
> The usual presence of Cupid
> The usual absence of style.
> A heroine brave and resourceful,
> Dread poisons, infernal machines,
> A hero alert and of course full
> Whenever they down him of beans.

Not even the splendid rhyme for 'resourceful' can bring me to forgive that ancient magazine for its libels.

I can, I suppose, forgive Graham Greene, who meant *Brighton Rock* to be a crime story before it got out of hand, however, for a very disparaging remark he once made about a favourite book of mine, Margery Allingham's *The Tiger in the Smoke*. After all, Greene was going up the mosquito-infested, heat-palpitating River Zaire when he read the book someone had lent him. But isn't he a bit harsh? 'A most absurd unreal story . . . It didn't even pass the time: it was an irritation.' Only for the love I bear that marvellous writer am I prepared to overlook his lapse.

But a comment by another novelist more or less of Greene's time, L.P. Hartley, I cannot overlook. 'What becomes of justice?' he wrote once in an essay called 'The Novelist's Responsibility'. 'Is it to be completely drowned in compassion? Detective stories have helped bring this about, and the convention that the murderee is always an unpleasant person, better out of the way.' Well, I know my addiction is a bit of a vice (how often have I let important matters slide while I attempted to discover who done it), but I don't really think our simple entertainment can be that guilty.

But, of course, the major indictment mystery fiction has had to face is an essay by the distinguished critic, Edmund Wilson, called

'Who Cares Who Killed Roger Ackroyd?'. It comes in his collection *Classics and Commercials: A Literary Chronicle of the Forties,* and downright nasty though it is about our patch of the literary landscape (the midden?), I must admit it's written with tremendous, even delightful, verve.

Mr Wilson begins by referring to an earlier newspaper article in which he had castigated a number of crime stories he had looked at, not having otherwise read any since his Sherlock Holmes days. That piece, he says, 'brought me letters of protest in a volume and of a passionate earnestness which had hardly been elicited even by my occasional criticisms of the Soviet Union'. In deference to the storm, he undertook to read books his correspondents had recommended, foremost among them Dorothy L. Sayers's *The Nine Tailors.*

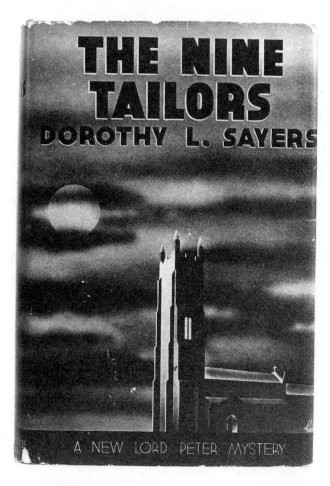

And here's what he had to say about that: 'It seems to me one of the dullest books I have ever encountered in any field.' The first part, he goes on, contains 'a lot of information of the kind you might expect to find in an encyclopedia article on campanology. I skipped a good deal of this.' Then he describes Lord Peter Wimsey as 'a dreadful stock English nobleman' and 'I had to skip a good deal of him, too.'

Lord Peter Wimsey

Well, I myself would not put the book among the very topmost of the field, though there are those who would. Indeed, it heads a list of the best ten compiled by Dr Erik Routley at the end of his thoughtful and interesting *The Puritan Pleasures of the Detective Story*. But I think Mr Wilson simply got hold of the wrong end of the stick.

Or even the wrong stick. He was looking for a novel. He should have been seeking a detective story. And a detective story, as I hope to show, is something that only looks like a novel proper – though since Mr Wilson produced his diatribe we have evolved something we could call the crime novel, something which at its best success-fully marries novel and detection.

So let me give you, and the shade of Mr Wilson (I refrain from saying where his lack of insight may have landed him), my case for the defence? Why do we really read crime?

First, a sociological explanation. Human beings are constrained to live in societies. Societies imply rules. Rules are, of necessity, restrictive. You must drive on the left (or on the right). But really we would like to drive right down the middle of the broad highway.

So, imagine then the storyteller under the palm tree or at the communal fire. What stories does he tell? Tales of a person, like yet unlike his listeners, who is able to defy laws they know they must submit to. He is the criminal, the arch-criminal even, hero of the Sensational Literature which Sherlock Holmes's knowledge of was reported by Dr Watson in *A Study in Scarlet* as being 'immense'.

But, no sooner have our imagined listeners under the palm tree felt a sense of release in hearing of this arch-criminal, the rules-free man, than they begin to think, 'Yes, but what if he robs *me*, rapes *me?*' So the teller of tales gives them the justicer, the man who can put things right. The Detective, long, long before his time, has been born.

In those pictures we see the two kinds of crime fiction in embryo, the upsetting and the reassuring, the school of Highsmith, the school of Christie. I can well recall a meeting of the judges for the annual Gold Dagger award of the Crime Writers Assocation at which the late Marghanita Laski threatened to resign if we gave the prize to the current Highsmith novel. (We didn't: but in the end we had felt something else was better.)

On the other hand, when I was editing a book called *Agatha Christie: First Lady of Crime* I asked Celia Fremlin (no mean writer in the upsetting tradition herself) to provide me with an essay on the reactions to Christie's writings over the years, and to complete the piece she interviewed various readers. One of them, a polytechnic teacher, said of her early days in a London bed-sitter: 'The one thing that made it endurable, going back to that awful little dark room in the evenings, was knowing that my Agatha Christies were waiting for me . . . People say that Agatha Christie characters are cardboard, but if they are, then cardboard friends were what I needed.'

So much for the sociological answer to the question, 'What is the attraction of crime?' But there is also a psychological explanation. It goes, broadly, as follows: Human beings require an optimum level of stimulation in their lives. This, of course, varies greatly between individuals and between various stages in an individual's life. It has been labelled a level of sensoristasis. Too little stimulation and we lose the necessary alertness to our surroundings; too much and we over-react.

And one way of adjusting our level of sensoristasis is by reading, with crime fiction perhaps the most efficient form of reading for this purpose. Over-stimulated, we should reach for our Christies; under-

THE BEDSIDE COMPANION TO CRIME

stimulated we should increase our level of beneficial awareness by swallowing a few chapters of Highsmith. It is a notion I find reasonably likely.

I find it so because I believe that fiction is more powerfully effective than your everyday reader might be willing to concede. Fiction is life re-arranged to bring out its fundamental attributes. Consequently, when these primal attributes are planted into our minds, it is hardly surprising we should be deeply affected. Fiction for this purpose is able to use what I call 'fiction-facts', that is, those authoritative statements by an author which do not correspond with the facts of existence in the world we live in. By re-interpreting that world using such invented 'facts' (invented usually and most effectively by the subconscious) a novelist makes more and more clear the underlying situations of our being.

Crime fiction, moreover, brings out these fundamentals to a larger extent than less form-based modes. The classical detective story, on which much crime fiction rests as a base, is in fact the fairy story. The detective is its knight errant. The murderer is its ogre. There are obstacles to be overcome. And we are always aware that they will be overcome, that there will be a happy-ever-after, and that we do but murder in jest. Fairy stories are, of course, myths. Myths, the most powerful reflections of our basic needs. Children, those basic human beings, respond to them strongly. We, more sophisticated, respond to them in the form of the crime story.

I go a little further, too, in my advocacy of crime fiction as a powerful and beneficial factor in life. When we read a novel proper which has perhaps been recommended to us as 'great' we are inclined to read with, so to speak, our hackles up. 'You have got something in your head you are determined to make me see,' we unconsciously address the author. 'Okay, but you're going to have to convince me, but good.' When one reads a crime story, however, one's guard is down. What one says to the author is merely 'Bet I can guess who done it before you tell me' or sometimes 'Hey, entertain me.'

And then if he or she wants to, the mystery novelist can slip in surreptitiously (appropriate method) a view he has or which she wants to put over of the way the world is.

Case rests.

10 LITTLE – WELL,
TEN LITTLE WHATS?

Easy to understand why when in 1939 Agatha Christie sent her American publisher a manuscript entitled *Ten Little Niggers*, which she had based as she delighted to do, on a rhyme she had learnt in the nursery, they blenched. 'Nigger' in America was a much dirtier word than it was at that time in England, innocently colour prejudiced and anti-semitic as it was in the days before World War II.

So, following an already well-established practice, the firm of Dodd, Mead, who published Agatha Christie from start to finish in the USA, altered that title. And in 1940 out in New York came *And Then There Were None*. A pretty good title, I would have thought. But by the time the book went into paperback in America someone had decided to make it *Ten Little Indians*, which was actually the title of a quite different rhyme written in 1964 in America by one Septimus Winner (he ought to have been Decimus with that decimal poem ahead of him).

But it was in 1931 that Dodd, Mead had begun their Christie mayhem. They altered *The Sittaford Mystery*, a plodding enough title, to *The Murder at Hazelmoor*, no less plodding. In 1933 *Lord Edgware Dies* became *Thirteen at Dinner* (and I thought Americans loved a lord). Next year *Why Didn't They Ask Evans?* (vital hint concealed in those words) became *The Boomerang Clue* and presumably American Christie fans thought she was taking them to Australia, whereas it was only the publisher who had got things upside down. Next, *Murder on the Orient Express* became *Murder in the Calais Coach*, though later film success reversed that. Indeed, the movie led eventually to an American-owned commercial success in Britain when that famous train was reconstituted (more or less) and an Orient Express once again swished its way from London at least as far as Venice.

Then *Murder in Three Acts* became *Three-Act Tragedy* (small improvement, I suppose) followed by *The A.B.C. Murders* becoming *The Alphabet Murders*. (All right, the train timetable *A.B.C.* was not American, but would the original title really have lost any Christie sales?) A few books survived after *Three-Act Tragedy* till 1937 when *Dumb Witness* became *Poirot Loses A Client*, on the grounds presumably that 'dumb' in America has an extra meaning to its basic one. But I suspect the Christie editor in America now looked at each title and thought, 'What can I alter here?'

So, having put Poirot into one title, when offered *Hercule Poirot's Christmas* they made it *Murder for Christmas* and even in paperback *A Holiday for Murder*. And, of course, *Murder Is Easy*, a title with real drawing power it seems to simple old me, became *Easy to Kill*. Then, in the same year as *And Then . . .*, 1940, appeared *One, Two, Buckle My Shoe*. Though the rhyme is familiar to Americans, it became first *The Patriotic Murders* and then, paperback transmogrification, *An Overdose of Death*, keeping up with the times a dozen years later.

Christie first thoughts survived for a little after that. But when she went back to her beloved nursery rhyme pattern with *Five Little Pigs*, though the rhyme is quoted and re-quoted throughout with even Belgian Hercule Poirot knowing it ('A jingle ran through Poirot's head. He repressed it. He must *not* always be thinking of nursery rhymes,' wrote Mrs Christie, tongue just in cheek) nevertheless stern New York decided on *Murder in Retrospect*. Why, though, three books later *Sparkling Cyanide* had to become *Remembered Death*, a title so near its predecessor, is anybody's guess. Or Dodd, Mead's.

Next *The Hollow* in paperback becomes *Murder After Hours* and right after that in hardback *Taken at the Flood* was made into a less apt part of the same quotation, *There Is A Tide . . .* Three survivors next. But then *They Do It With Mirrors* became *Murder With Mirrors* probably because someone in New York had a dirtier mind than the future Dame Agatha.

In 1952 it was back to the old unwillingness to allow any of those Christie nursery rhymes, and *Mrs McGinty's Dead* (again quoted in the pages) became the feeble *Blood Will Tell*. Next year *After the Funeral* was altered to the cruder *Funerals Are Fatal*, though back on the British side of the giant pond, thanks to a film strictly for local consumption, that book ended up, in an unlikely fashion, as a paperback *Murder At The Gallop*. However, in 1953 Mrs Christie produced a nursery rhyme title which actually survived its Atlantic voyage, remaining in New York in 1954 *A Pocket Full of Rye*, though

Agatha Christie photographed by Angus McBean.

Hercule Poirot.

surely some would-be readers must have wondered how the drink managed to stay in that pocket.

Destination Unknown the following year had, of course, of course, to be re-titled *So Many Steps to Death*, and its successor book, another rhyme, went from *Hickory, Dickory, Dock* to *Hickory, Dickory, Death*. Rather more reason to make *4.50 From Paddington* into *What Mrs McGillycuddy Saw!*, though the pocket book people thought *Murder She Said* preferable. I might have made it *Murder She Saw*, but no matter. And in any case I would have thought that by this stage the great Christean zoom of popularity would have sold the book had it been called just *Christie's 50th*.

16

And it seems that the message was, in fact, beginning to get through because, beyond dropping the last four words of *The Mirror Crack'd From Side to Side* (poor old Tennyson), thereafter Dodd, Mead let each Christie title make that perilous ocean crossing unscathed, right up to *Sleeping Murder*, her 1976 farewell.

Yet I suppose Dame Agatha was to an extent lucky. At least the words she wrote inside the covers got to be sacrosanct. But not all Atlantic crossing authors are so safe from alteration. Read on.

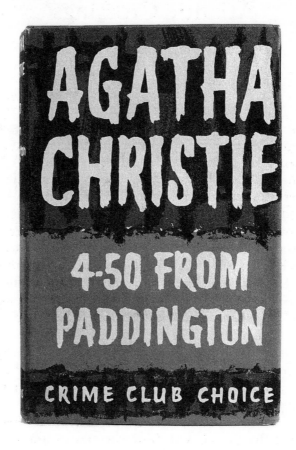

9 SLY GLANCES

Atlantic Crossings

Not only do Agatha Christie titles get changed when they make the crossing of the great Atlantic Ocean. Other curious things happen to books. It's not only the way American civilisation often sees things differently from the British, or the other way round. Yes, Patricia Highsmith has a much higher reputation in Britain, and an even higher one in translation in Europe, than she seems to have in her native United States. And, yes, Gladys Mitchell, though hailed in England by our esteemed poet Philip Larkin, as 'the great Gladys', has a hard time even seeing the light of day in America. And, yes again, transversely (*mot juste*) for some reason America's much-praised Jane Langton who, she says, actually began writing mysteries 'under the spell of Dorothy L. Sayers', is unseen in Britain. But it is the odder, if perhaps less portentous, things that happen over the Atlantic that intrigue me.

Chiefly it is in the way titles change. One can see why Michael Innes's *Death at the President's Lodging* had to become in America *Seven Suspects*, a title actually once suggested for the affair by one of the book's characters. But why, one wonders, did it have to make a return voyage and be *Seven Suspects* in Britain? (The answer, dully commercial, is that it was somehow cheaper to import American paperbacks than to produce a different British version.) But some other new American titles surely raise an eyebrow or two.

Ngaio Marsh's *Surfeit of Lampreys*, that favourite book of hundreds of readers, appeared first in America, for instance, as dullissimo *Death of a Peer*. All right, citizens of the great republic are notorious for loving a lord but equally they are taught, for the most part and oddly, British history up to the time America received its whitewash.

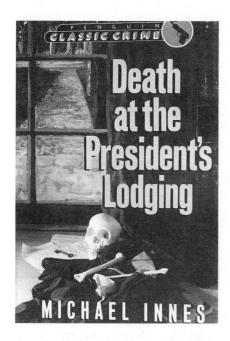

So readers of books as mildly demanding as Miss Marsh's surely ought to have known about poor old, bad old King John – actually he tried to be Good but circs, as they usually are, were against him – and the way he died of a surfeit of cyclostomes, thus giving Miss Marsh a wonderful name to disguise the dizzy family of English eccentrics she had encountered in her native New Zealand when she put them, lockish, stockish and barrelish, into her tenth detective story.

On the other hand, it is not easy to see why John Dickson Carr's *The Three Coffins*, with its three parts labelled by him 'First Coffin', 'Second Coffin' and 'Third Coffin', should have been called *The Hollow Man* when it crossed from Carr's America to Britain, though Carr does thus describe his 'impossible' murder in the book. Certainly the double titling has caused more than a little trouble, in the way of frequent bracketed explanations, to those of us crime commentators wishing to recommend to readers on both sides of the Atlantic its Chapter 17 as a definitive guide to how to do the hermetically sealed chamber one. I suppose, though, the United States can be said to have had its revenge nearly 40 years later over another 'coffin' title. In 1973 Gwendoline Butler's delightful story of Victorian Oxford, *A Coffin for Pandora* came out in New York as

Olivia, not exactly a must-read title, followed by *A Coffin for the Canary* becoming *Sarsen Place,* and yet duller, the highly romantic *The Brides of Friedberg* being reduced to *Meadowsweet.* 'I don't know why,' Gwen said to me plaintively.

It was in 1935, the year of *The Three Coffins,* too, that America played foul with one of the detective stories, now largely and rather undeservedly forgotten, of Georgette Heyer, the novelist of Regency rakes. In Britain Miss Heyer entitled her book, accurately if not with startling originality, *Death in the Stocks,* since her body was to be discovered in the ancient village stocks of Ashleigh Green. All right, stocks in America in the aftermath of the Wall Street crash might not at first bring to mind that wooden medieval instrument of public punishment and humiliation. But it would be a dull crime fan indeed who did not feel a tingle of excitement at the thought of a corpse among the company registers. So what had Miss Heyer's American publishers got to lose? Well, they called the book *Merely Murder.* Enough said.

However, let us acknowledge that on some occasions American publishers sparked up much better titles than their British counterparts. Indeed, a now lost-in-time (unjustly) book, which was called in England *The Vicar's Experiments* but was in Boston re-named *Clerical Error,* later adopted the brilliant pun in its country of origin. The book first appeared, on both sides of the Atlantic, as by Anthony Rolls. But this pseudonym has been revealed as that of C.E. Vulliamy, who under his own name produced, 20 years after *Clerical Error,* in 1952, a pretty good pun title of his own, *Don Among the Dead Men.*

It may have been a very successful cover that was responsible for an Atlantic title change to what has become a crime classic of equal stature to *The Three Coffins,* E.C. Bentley's *Trent's Last Case* (written, so its author claimed, to show up the detective story, but boomeranging into detectival stardom). Published in England in 1913 with a cover and frontispiece picture of its widow chief suspect dressed all in black, a striking drawing indeed, it came out originally in America as simply *The Woman in Black.* And thus brought yet more complications for crime historians.

Another paradoxical beneficiary of Atlantean title change is Peter Dickinson. In 1968, having written children's books and been assistant editor of *Punch,* he produced a first detective novel, so good that it won him the Gold Dagger of the Crime Writers Association. He wanted to call the book *The Glass-sided Ants' Nest,* a nicely odd title and one that well reflected the superbly bizarre setting, a tribe

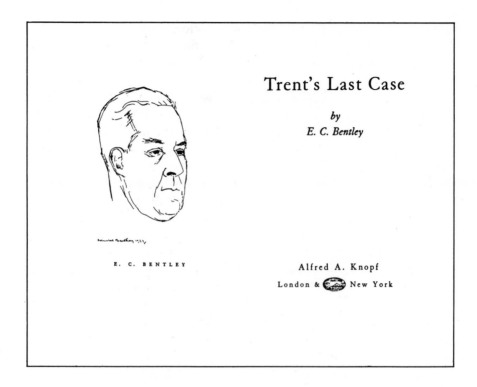

Trent's Last Case

by
E. C. Bentley

E. C. BENTLEY

Alfred A. Knopf

London & New York

of New Guinea primitives transported en bloc by an anthropologist to the attics of a row of London houses.

But at Peter Dickinson's British publishing house there was an old, old man, learned beyond steeping in publishing lore. And this ancient decreed that 'No book with an insect in the title ever goes'. I was myself in 1963 a victim of that same theory when a book I had called *A Worm for His Brain* had that title condemned out of hand by the late, great publisher Victor Gollancz. We hit instead on *The Dog It Was That Died*, and I had hastily to write in a part for a dog. Similarly, in consultation with Peter Dickinson another title was found for his book, *Skin Deep*. But in whizz-bang, go-ahead America such insect superstitions were unheard of. So there *Skin Deep* was called what its author had originally intended. And recently, floating back across the ocean, it has come as a Penguin – called *The Glass-sided Ants' Nest*.

Peter Dickinson's second crime story, which also won a Gold Dagger – unrepeated feat – and was called in Britain by his chosen title, *A Pride of Heroes*, suffered, however, that same old sea-change. In America it became *The Old English Peep Show*, and, indeed, his

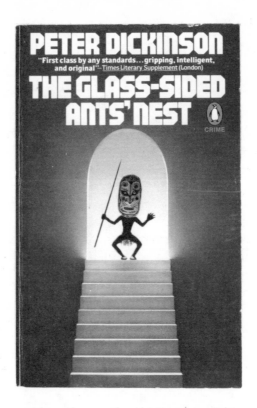

next, which I remember, sitting on the judging panel, as nearly gaining a third Gold Dagger, *The Seals*, also suffered that change to become *The Sinful Stones* – pretty catchpenny or, I suppose one might say, catchcent.

Yet perhaps the strangest thing to happen to a crime book as it winged its way over the vast Atlantic occurred to the second novel June Thomson wrote. Her first, *Not One of Us*, for which she invented that likeable, credible, East Anglian policeman, Detective Inspector Finch, travelled across to America in 1971, a year before its British publication, totally intact, to be published by Harper. However, Finch's second investigation in 1973, *Death Cap*, did not come out in America until 1977, when it was published by Doubleday. And Doubleday insisted, for reasons never quite clear to Mrs Thomson, that Inspector Finch become Inspector Rudd. So to this day he has remained: Finch to British readers, Rudd to American. And how disconcerted you would be if your career happened to take you at some stage, as many do, from one side of the ocean to the other.

Is They Is, Or Are They Ain't?

Crime fans, and crime commentators, are very apt to seize on any novel, preferably by a great writer, and claim it as theirs. Had poor old Dostoyevsky been granted a vision of the crime-writing flood of our century, would he have hastily revised his title *Crime and Punishment*, aware of how many times that deep and colossal work (which does contain a murder) would be claimed as somehow justifying a taste for such possibly pleasant trivia as *Death on the Borough Council* or *End of A Call Girl*?

Nobel-winner Faulkner is another often claimed for crime, and, of course, if you do no more than lay out the bare bones of *Sanctuary* or *Intruder in the Dust* they can well be made to look like common-or-garden mystery books. Faulkner was, in fact, a great reader and even admirer of the detective novel with John Dickson Carr, Rex Stout, Agatha Christie and Dorothy L. Sayers found on his library shelves at his death. More, he once won second prize in a contest organised by *Ellery Queen's Mystery Magazine* with a short story called 'An Error in Chemistry'. But it is too much, really, to claim that in any of his novels he was doing no more than spin a mystery puzzle.

Graham Greene is yet another who has not escaped the trap-net of the mad mystery fancier. And certainly it is not altogether easy to say what it is in *The Human Factor* that distinguishes it from – well, let us say, any good spy novel produced at round about the same time. Except that it is better, goes more deeply into the human condition, is written with more concealed power, as were even those early thrillers Greene once labelled 'entertainments'. In an article on Greene in that splendid tome *Twentieth Century Crime and Mystery Writers*, the distinguished biographer, George Woodcock, making the sort of claim often made by crime buffs, eventually gives the game away by saying, 'It is at this point that crime shades off into sin.' When sin takes precedence as it surely does in such books as *The Ministry of Fear*, *This Gun for Hire*, *The Third Man* and *Brighton Rock*, one could say, crime loses its claim.

That much said, there are a fair number of novelists proper who have occasionally descended to crime, often alas condescended to crime. My best remembered of these latter is C.P. Snow, the novelist

23

of academe and Civil Service power struggles. I do not rate even these as high as many critics, but I think his late entry into crime, *A Coat of Varnish*, written in 1979, a year before his death, is almost universally recognised as being a ponderous bore. His very first venture into fiction, a whodunit, *Death Under Sail*, in 1932 is at least up to snuff for its day, though it's significant, I think, that the 26-year-old author chose a narrator of 62. Snow's wife, Pamela Hansford Johnson, a sharper novelist, also descended to crime in her early days in collaboration with her first husband, Gordon Stewart. They produced in 1940 and 1942 *Tidy Death* and *Murder's A Swine* under the pseudonym, which in itself ought to get them readers, of Nap Lombard. And their sleuth, Lord Winterstone, was promisingly also known as Lord Pig.

But of Arnold Bennett, he of the *Five Towns* novels and post-humous second fame on television, as crime writer there is little good to say. Julian Symons, to whose ever-interesting literary history *Bloody Murder* or *Mortal Consequences* I am indebted for putting Nap Lombard on my long unread reading-list, calls Bennett's *Buried Alive* 'a ridiculous novel' and says *The Grand Babylon Hotel* is 'almost equally absurd'. Two not for my reading-list. And I am unlikely to get my hands on a third Bennett crime foray, *The Loot of Cities*: it is one of the rarest first editions of twentieth-century book-collecting, though it has been reprinted in America.

Nor, I think, will I put on to my list any out of the enormous fiction output of J.B. Priestley that can be claimed for crime, much pleasure though I once got out of his *The Good Companions*. Most of his half-dozen entries into the genre are espionage tales, but *Salt Is Leaving* was described by its publisher in 1966 as 'a pungent novel of crime and detection'. On the other hand, that publisher was simply a British paperback house and the book had to wait till 1975 before an American hardback house would take it on.

Some novelists, however, can be seen as stepping up when they turn to crime. Or so at least Julian Symons says of Hugh Walpole – Sir Hugh, knighted novelist – whose work in general he castigates as 'saccharine'. But certainly Walpole's single crime novel, *Above the Dark Circus*, is a powerful, fear-permeated book. Written in 1931, it was revived to some critical acclaim in 1985.

Another novelist who contrived a high standard during a tempo-rary side-step into the mystery field was Gore Vidal. In the 1950s, long before *Burr* and *Lincoln*, he wrote three mysteries under the pseudonym of Edgar Box. They have been labelled mediocre as formal detective stories, but *Death in the Fifth Position*, *Death Before Bedtime* and *Death Likes It Hot*, hintingly salacious titles, all zing with sharp satire.

Another literary giant who stepped down once to a murder mystery – I by no means guarantee to record the lot – was Rudyard Kipling. He has one, at least, fine murder story, 'Mary Postgate', but a murder story is altogether different from a murder mystery story and always a good deal more serious. However, Kipling did once send to the *Strand Magazine*, its first success owed to Conan Doyle and Sherlock Holmes, a very neatly told and not altogether trivial mystery story set in the aftermath of World War I called 'Fairy Kist'. And I suppose one might tag on to Kipling a less mighty but still excellent writer, C.S. Forester, chronicler of the sea adventures of Horatio Hornblower. His first book, *Payment Deferred*, in 1926 was a decidedly gripping crime story of a surburban bank clerk who murders his Australian nephew for his money but then succumbs to the dictates of his conscience, an early example of what is called the 'inverted' mystery. *Plain Murder* in 1930 was of the same sort, if not so free of unlikelinesses.

Which brings me to a novel with in it only the unlikelinesses of real life, Francis King's reconstruction of the Constance Kent murder case of 1860 set in twentieth-century India and England, *Act of Darkness*. This is, to my mind, clearly a novel proper in that it deals with evil and sin. But, in that it is a splendid mystery as well, one might, in this instance, allow that a book can be both novel and crime novel.

From Francis King's novel of 1983 let us leap back to the days when to all intents and purposes there was no crime fiction except for such fiction that was part of the great rushing stream and happened to be about crime. From that torrent let us pluck out one book that, but for fate, might have been at the outset an absolute example of the work of fiction that at equal levels is both crime novel and plain novel, Charles Dickens's unfinished, vibrant with life *The Mystery of Edwin Drood*.

Challenged by the success of his friend Wilkie Collins with *The Moonstone*, Dickens launched into a similar work. He chose for it a story that gave promise of being as good a puzzle as could be imagined, the mysterious disappearance from the quiet cathedral town of Cloisterham of one Edwin Drood – the puzzle has kept commentators and would-be concluders of the unconcluded busy ever since – and alongside that he found a theme, the frightening

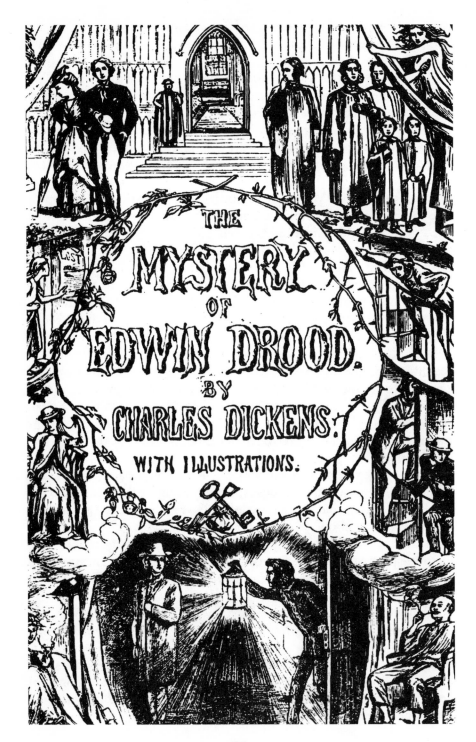

duality of our human nature, that ever-raging combat of duty and desire, fit to power any novel you choose to name.

The book was never finished. Death stilled the writer's pen. I think one of the most heart-touching sights I have ever seen was the original manuscript in a London exhibition, with its sad concluding words '. . . and then falls to with an appetite.' Perhaps cruel fate meant us never to fall to with an appetite on a book simultaneously wholly major crime novel and wholly major novel. Or is that day still to come?

Errors and Omissions

I don't much like reading manuscripts for publishers. They never ask you to do this when they have got a real humdinger from a new author on their hands, only when they are filled with doubts. So one is generally in the position of having to say unpleasant things, however unpublished, about the work of a fellow writer. But one such manuscript I treasure in my memory. I have a notion it must have been submitted by a friend of a friend of the publisher (I do not treasure the memory of his identity) and what was wanted from me was what would look like an unbiased comment saying the book was not publishable.

It was, in fact, pretty dire. But the moment in it I have never forgotten was when the hero, whom the author had striven to make a complete man-of-the-world, strode into a night club, ordered a magnum of champagne, swigged it down and left, seemingly steady on his feet, with the equivalent of two solid bottles of bubbly doing their damndest inside him.

But we all make mistakes, and our editors do not always come to the rescue before they are immortalised on the page. It is then that one is apt to get what I call a 'But' letter. A 'But' letter begins with some acknowledgement of having liked your book, and then comes 'But . . .' Generally, I am happy to say, the 'but' refers to some

BELOVED BUNGLERS

Not every detective is as all-conquering as Sherlock
Holmes (and he was defeated by Irene Adler, *the*
Woman). Indeed, my own Inspector Ghote has been
referred to as 'that endearing bungler'. We both resent that
final word.

But I doubt if Joyce Porter resents any similar
description of her Chief Inspector Wilfred Dover, who has
always solved his cases by a mixture of luck and taking
advantage of the work and ideas of others, with occasional
accesses of shrewdness which just overcome his congenital
laziness, his problems with his digestion and his fearful
greed. He is reputed to have got on to the Murder Squad
because no one else would have him, a parallel case
perhaps to Ed McBain's 87th Precinct stupid, Dick
Genero, promoted by accident.

I suppose 'bungler' is not the exact word for the
detective created by the humorists Caryl Brahms and S.J.
Simon, Inspector Adam Quill, in three books written
between 1937 and 1940. Quill never solved a single case.
But this was because the murderers *would* confess to him
before he had a chance to detect them.

Charles Paris, Simon Brett's actor-sleuth, does,
however, manage to bring to justice the various villains he
encounters as chance takes him into different areas of the
theatrical profession in Britain. Yet he seems to proceed
almost always in a hideously unprofessional way. His
acting, poor fellow, though much more professional,
brings him almost equal ill-luck. But that's what makes
him so nice to read about.

No prizes in the dumbo stakes. But, if a prize was going,
a fair claimant might be Philo Gubb, hero of comic stories
written by Ellis Parker Butler in America in the early years
of this century and published in a book *Philo Gubb* in
1918. Philo was a 'correspondence school detective' and
had a huge range of disguises. Not one of which ever
deceived anybody. But he could be closely rivalled by
James Powell's Acting-Sergeant Ballard of the Canadian
Mounties: his creator said of him he is 'an earnest bungler
of whom I am unashamedly fond'. That's talking.

personal quirk of the letter writer's, such as in my case when I have been incautious enough to indicate where in India my murderer comes from, 'the well-known fact' that no Gujarati or Maharashtrian or Bengali or Madrasi, as the case may be, has ever been known to commit any crime, much less murder.

However, one morning I received a note from a Mrs May Storey, of Fareham, Hampshire, which began (I knew the signs, though) 'I have just finished *Inspector Ghote Draws A Line* and found it so enjoyable that I made it last out four evenings instead of racing to find the solution.' And then it came, the 'But'. 'My chief reason for writing to you is to point out a very amusing slight error on page 36. The old Judge is given a Picasso appearance ". . . saw the sunken eyes between the Judge's oddly flattened nose." ' Well, yes, you are absolutely right, Mrs Storey. Picasso is the word. I had perpetrated a fairly astonishing error – together with everyone who read the typescript before publication.

Of course, the greatest risk of putting into print some gross error is when one ventures into any field of expertise, with perhaps the most dangerous being trains and railways. The rail buff lurks, hands rubbing. I once put Inspector Ghote on a train going from Bombay all the way across India to Calcutta. Lots of nice local colour, I thought. The romance of Indian railways. Fair enough. But, to give a feeling of progress to my train, I listed the names of the stations through which it passed as it left Bombay. I had the map in front of me, with them all marked. But. All the way from India came the train buff's letter. 'You have written Sandhurst Road High Level, but it is well known that the Calcutta train is passing through Sandhurst Road Low Level.' I hung my head in shame.

I am glad to find I am not alone in making railway errors, however. Turn to one of those mysteries written by the American Martha Grimes and set in England, hailed by American reviewers as marvellously typical, *The Old Fox Deceiv'd*. (Ms Grimes charmingly gives each of her books a title that is also a genuine British pub name.) And there you will find her astute Scotland Yard man setting off for York by going to Victoria Station in London. Well, I suppose he might go south to one of the Channel ports, proceed across Europe and down the Suez Canal to India, and on round the world till at last he could descend from somewhere in the region of the Arctic to that ancient city in the north of England where lies the vital clue.

One of the pleasures for a Briton in reading the Grimes books is, indeed, the logging of little errors. Mostly they are of speech, such

Martha Grimes.

as the man who sits reading *The Times* in 'vest and suspenders (waistcoat and braces, Ms Grimes). I point that out only because of the much more embarrassing error I myself just avoided making by asking kind Patricia Highsmith to look at the typescript of a book with an American in it before I sent it to my publisher. She wrote back, considerably amused. I had had my American 'knocking up' a girl, making her pregnant, poor lady, when all I had thought he was doing was tapping at her door early in the morning.

But even the kings and queens of crime are liable to fall foul of lurking error. As witness Dorothy L. Sayers who incautiously entered the closed world of bell-ringing in *The Nine Tailors* on the strength of a sixpenny pamphlet picked up by chance – and invented a method of killing which would not produce death, as well as breaking a fundamental rule of that esoteric art by allowing a relief ringer to take part in her famous nine-hour champion peal.

Earlier, in *Unnatural Death*, she had invented a murder method that is appropriately dramatic and cunningly ingenious, the injection of an air-bubble with a hypodermic, but not only, in fact, would it require the use of an instrument so large as to be farcical, but Miss Sayers has her bubble put into an artery not a vein. No wonder afterwards she pledged herself 'strictly in future to seeing I never write a book which I know to be careless'. But that was before she produced *The Nine Tailors*.

Wrong Again

Arthur Upfield, creator of the Australian outback detective, Napoleon Bonaparte (commonly called Bony) in 29 books written between 1929 and 1966, is one of those crime authors who has survived on the shelves and seems likely to go on doing so. And this despite the fact that as a writer he is a great purveyor of ponderous prose.

He has, however, two considerable virtues that outweigh that disadvantage. He told a good, ongoing story, and he set most of his books in that unusual background which he knew with the intimacy of a lover. Little wonder then that he is still popular, especially in the United States where there is even a 'fanzine' in his honour, *The Bony Bulletin*, edited by Philip T. Asdell, to whom I owe some of what I know about Upfield..

Upfield was, in fact, lucky to become an Australian writer. Born in 1888 (I write these words just a few days after his exact centenary of 1 September) in Hampshire, the eldest of the five sons of a draper, he showed little aptitude for the work of the estate agent to whom he was apprenticed, though he had produced before he was 16 a novel, never published, of some 100,000 words. At the age of 19 he was packed off by his irate father to distant Australia. There he became a boundary rider inspecting fences for lonely mile after lonely mile, a camp cook and a sheep-herder and, after war service in

1914, he was a fur trapper, an opal hunter and a gold miner. All gave him experiences he was later to make good use of.

But it was another piece of luck that set him on the road to fame. He had written a book, called *The Barrakee Mystery*, which had failed to find a publisher. Undeterred, he wrote *The House of Cain*, a thriller that did see print. Then one day a half-caste called Tracker Leon happened to ride into the camp where Upfield was working and so enthralled the young Englishman with his tales of working for the Queensland Police that he took his rejected *Barrakee* manuscript and made its detective a figure based on Leon but romanticised up.

He decided his hero, besides possessing Tracker Leon's extraordinary skills, should have been found as an abandoned baby, evidently the offspring of a white man and an aborigine mother, attempting to eat a book, the life of the great French emperor. Hence the name that was bestowed on him. From his mixed ancestry Bony inherited the European's gift of what Edgar Allan Poe called 'rationalisation' and from his native Australian mother he got the strong intuition which supplies an opposite strain. So he could become a Great Detective, in the mould of Poe's Dupin, solving mysteries by rising to conclusions that transcended both the opposing ways of thinking.

Now *The Barrakee Mystery* gained a publisher, and off Upfield went with successors to it year by year, though not all of them in the early days actually featured his new hero. However, the second Bony book, *The Sands of Windee*, brought about a real-life story as astonishing as any of the Upfield fictions.

Upfield himself eventually told the story in a small paperback, *The Murchison Murders*, only some 64 pages long. It was published in Australia in 1934, and has been recently re-discovered by an Australian Bonyist (if that is the right word), Bill Miller.

For *The Sands of Windee* Upfield had found a tremendously ingenious plot. There was to be a murder without a body, and only brilliant Bony would be able to prove murder had been committed in the first place and, later, who it was who had committed it. But, first difficulty, how to get rid of a body completely in the land-locked Australian outback. For months Upfield posed this question to everyone he chanced to meet. Eventually he was given the solution by the manager of a camel station at which he was staying. It was a complicated business involving burning the corpse, reducing the ashes to powder and then adding them to the ashes of a bush fire. But it seemed foolproof. Upfield used it in the book he came to write.

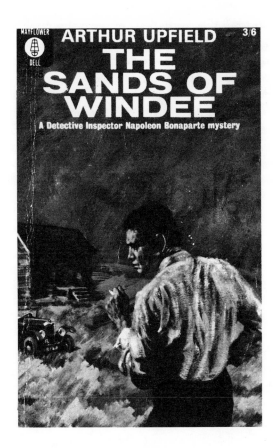

But, when discussing it round the fire at the camel station, a man called Snowy Rolls had also taken part in the talk. And he decided to put the method to real use. Taking advantage of the fact that station-hands frequently carried large sums in paid-out wages and that they were also apt to go from station to station and thus would not be likely to be missed, Snowy Rolls killed three men. Only after his murders did Upfield's book, demonstrating how to do it, come out. But Snowy Rolls was seen to be unusually flush with money and was arrested. At this trial Arthur Upfield was a key witness.

So far so dramatic. But later commentators, all unknowing of Upfield's little book about the business, were unable to resist a certain amount of embroidery. So eventually it was stated, with all the authority of the printed word, that it was actually one of Snowy Roll's victims who had suggested the murder method to Arthur Upfield and that Rolls had had a copy of *The Sands of Windee* and had used it as a sort of manual, leaving it near the site of the bush fire where he had hidden the human ashes with the vital four pages torn out. It was, this account says, Upfield himself, worriedly investigating, who found the partly burnt copy. It was the case of the man who solved his own murder. Big romantic deal.

And who was it who put all this tosh once more into print? H.R.F. Keating in his *Crime and Mystery: the 100 Best Books*, basing himself on a wrong-headed magazine article and all unconscious when he wrote of Upfield's own more prosaic account of the affair.

The Duller the Better

When I was for a short time crime books reviewer for the *Daily Telegraph* I wrote a piece that began 'Hail the dull' and went on to praise with that faint damn Sara Woods's books about Anthony Maitland QC, his solved crimes and courtroom battles. It got me into a little trouble, but I still think my justification of the dull holds good.

One of the main reasons for reading crime fiction, I said then more or less, is so as to acquire an all-embracing feeling of comfort. That can come, I suggested, not just from the fact that at the end of a crime story written in the classical detection mode you know you are going to see justice done, something that in the often ugly real world we cannot always be sure of. But that comfort comes, too, from pages of smoothly undisturbed writing, and it was with that I credited Sara Woods, whose final posthumous book, *Naked Villainy*, I was reviewing, last of nearly 50 beginning in 1962 with *Bloody Instructions*. (William Shakespeare kindly provided Sara Woods with the majority of her murderous titles.)

I went on in that same review to bracket Sara Woods with M.G. Eberhart, known in her native America as Mignon G., whose 58th book, *A Fighting Chance*, was then also, as they say, to hand. And, though Ms Eberhart had a much more varied output than Ms Woods, a lot of what I praised in dullness applies to her later books

NOT THE END

John Rhode, stalwart of the detective story's Golden Age, would on occasion finish a book with the thumpingly ferocious words '. . . and he was duly hanged.' After which he would write, as they generally did in those days, THE END. Just so as you were sure. Raymond Chandler, on the other hand, once suggested that the 'ideal mystery' was 'one you would read if the end was missing'. A thought that requires some pondering. Consider it in the light of some words of a rather different writer, Mickey Spillane. His formula for success: 'You don't read a book to get to the middle. You read it to get to the end.'

Whatever the merits of that, getting to the end as a mystery writer was something that defeated the American novelist, Harold Brodsky. Not only was his novel proper *Party of Animals* still unfinished after 30 years' work, but when he was contracted to write a murder story he abandoned the idea after, he says, he had got to page 700 'and no one was dead yet'.

Sometimes, alas, a book is unfinished because the author's life has come to end. A case in point was Margery Allingham's *A Cargo of Eagles.* This did eventually appear, in 1968, completed by her husband, the illustrator Philip Youngman Carter. Sadly, his hand shows. All the Allingham joyous bizarreness is there in outline, but somehow the little different words that would have set it aflame are missing. Reviewing it those many years ago, I wrote: 'The aspic is cloudily thick – though under it you can just see the firm outline of the delectable quail, but, alas, the *maitre d'hôtel* who would have deftly removed all but a moistening trace of the jelly has left the restaurant for ever.'

I would much like to read another example of a book finished by a different hand, but it's hard to find. When in 1899 Grant Allen, prolific crime novelist and story-writer and author of a book that caused much scandal in its day, *The Woman Who Did*, died his neighbour, Conan Doyle, finished the last chapter of *Hilda Wade: A Woman of Great Tenacity of Purpose.* Snappy title.

and not even the exotic locales she used in the 1960s make her books exciting in the way, say, Hammett's are. But then often excitement is not what we want in crime. Agatha Christie, indeed, earned much of her immense popularity through her share of delightful dullness.

I got into more trouble over this dullness business recently when a reader came across the introduction I had written for a reprint of John Rhode's detective story of 1933, *The Claverton Mystery*, one of a series called 'The Disappearing Detectives' I selected for Collins Crime Club, picking out sleuths from the past who had become more or less lost to view.

Writing about Rhode and his Dr Priestley I incautiously said of an earlier title, *The Paddington Mystery*, that it was dull, and I also categorised most of the books that Major Cecil Street wrote either as Rhode (78 of these) or as Miles Burton (a mere 63) as 'astonishingly dull'. But not even the citing of the opinion of those learned crime connoisseurs, Professor Jacques Barzun and Wendell Hertig Taylor, that some of the Rhode books were 'beyond belief dull' and 'well-nigh unreadable' could save me from the wrath of Mr Peter Ibbotson of Bournemouth, once a friend of Major Street.

'Do you – or others who have levelled the charge "dull" – really think,' Mr Ibbotson thundered, 'that a publisher would have continued . . . to publish the books of an author who was dull? Would people have continued to buy and read the books of an author who was dull?' Well, yes, sir, that really is my point. Dull, nicely dull, books are what we the reading public want for a great deal of the time.

When Rhodes and Burtons were coming out in that thick and fast stream – and, remember, this was in the days when there was no anodyne, samey television to fill the vital task of keeping us just awake in the evenings – the books of Freeman Wills Crofts, whom Julian Symons in his magisterial *Bloody Murder* or *Mortal Consequences* calls the best representative of the 'Humdrum school', were also there to be borrowed from the circulating libraries, together with those of G.D.H. and Margaret Cole, who though startlingly lively as socialist academics, had hit squarely on the idea that what the detective-story reader wanted was simple brick by brick storytelling plus the lure of that wonderful question, 'Who done it?' The Coles's Superintendent Henry Wilson is described in *Twentieth Century Crime and Mystery Writers* as 'one of the most colourless detectives ever invented'.

Bracketed with the Coles one could surely place E.R. Punshon, now almost entirely forgotten, but a staple of my boyhood reading and of countless detection fans in the 1930s and on into the 1940s and 1950s. Let me quote at random a chunk from his 1937 book, *Mystery of Mr Jessop* (and there, damn it, is another good and dull title).

> His thoughts turned again to the minor point of how it was that the duke knew that Jessop gambled for large sums. Fisher – that had been a useful little chat – denied that his master went often to the races, and in any case it was not likely the duke would have there noticed, or paid the least attention to, Mr Jessop's activities, or, indeed, had any opportunity to do so, since there was no reason why the duke and the jeweller should have seen each other, even though both had been on the same racecourse the same day.

Compare and contrast any quarter page of Raymond Chandler, who once said of mystery merchants, 'the English may not be the best writers in the world but they are incomparably the best dull writers'.

Who Killed Round Robin?

In those days in the history of the mystery when fun filled the pages, between, if you like, the essential seriousness of Sherlock Holmes and the moment when Chandler deified the 'mean streets', in the days when solving the puzzle was, in the words of John Dickson Carr, 'the grandest game in the world', there arose a phenomenon.

Since ingenuity was the thing, it occurred to one Sir Max Pemberton in the year 1914 that you could multiply ingenuity simply by multiplying the number of authors for any one story. So he devised a thickly mysterious murder and invited a clutch of celebrities to contribute their solutions to *The Premier* magazine. Who most of them were it would take a detective more probingly painstaking than myself to discover. But one of them I do know, since the story he contributed has been reprinted. It is G.K. Chesterton who allowed

RED HERRINGS

Red herrings, these ingenious deceitful by-paths so beloved of the constructors of the classical detective story, are in fact the dried, smoked and salted fish which were dragged across the path of a hunted fox to set the hounds at fault out of sheer mischief in the good old days. Now, similar tricks are played, out of immense high-mindedness, by the ecological hunt saboteurs who roam England's green fields.

The King of Herrings, be it noted, is a fish that often accompanies shoals of herring. It is also known as the sea-ape and as the Chimaera, a chimaera being classically not a sea-ape but a she-goat, a fabulous monster in Greek mythology with (Homer says so: it must be right) a lion's head, a dragon's tail and a goat's body. A chimaera means, in English, a wild incongruous scheme. A good many of those seem, too, to inhabit the realms of crime fiction.

Dorothy L. Sayers' *The Five Red Herrings* must be the book that provides the best examples of that ilk, though it is hardly her most successful novel. In fact, her first biographer, Janet Hitchman, said, 'It commits the unpardonable sin in a detective work of being exceedingly dull.' Nor did Miss Sayers find that title all that easily. She wanted to call the book *Six Suspects*, but thought that had been used. She toyed with *Six Unlikely Persons*. She rejected *The Body in the Burn* as 'dull', and even considered *There's One Thing Missing* with a blank paragraph where Lord Peter would tell the local sergeant what that something was and how important it would be. Victor Gollancz, her publisher, said 'No.'

Finally, the journal of the Crime Writers Association is called – well, it had to be called something – *Red Herrings*.

his Father Brown to take something of a holiday by participating in *The Donnington Affair*. His effort reads oddly on its own without the key facts laid out first, but there are some nice flashes of the wisdom of Father Brown in it, such as 'The man she wronged most was a man who had never had, or tried to have, more than one virtue – a kind of acrid justice.'

But in this way there was born the round-robin detective story. It was a puling infant, and born at a bad time with World War I just looming. So it is hardly surprising that we hear little more of it until in 1930 the newly formed Detection Club in London set out to acquire some funds.

They did this by writing two serials for radio, or the wireless as it was called in those days. These were not plays but a pair of stories written and read by various authors. *Behind the Screen* was immediately printed in *The Listener* magazine and a prize was offered for the best answers to questions put by the club member, detective novelist and reviewer, Milward Kennedy. The first three collaborators in this venture, Dorothy L. Sayers, Agatha Christie and Hugh Walpole (whose flirtation with crime fiction had gained him admission to the club) wrote in the spirit of the greatest fun, popping in whatever their fancy suggested – a housekeeper called Mrs Hulk, an aspidistra . . .

The three remaining authors were Anthony Berkeley, creator of Roger Sheringham and later as Francis Iles to canonise the inverted mystery; E.C. Bentley, author of *Trent's Last Case*; and Ronald Knox, at that time chaplain to the Roman Catholic students at Oxford. *The Scoop*, set in a newspaper office, broadcast in 1931, was started by Dorothy L. Sayers and wound up, rather sternly, by Freeman Wills Crofts.

The two radio ventures were successful enough for the Detection Club to try again, still in 1931, with a round-robin story designed to become a book, *The Floating Admiral*. This did so well on re-publication 50 years later that it brought the club a large access of funds, by then needed once more. Among the cherished items in the club library now is the German edition, *Der Admirals Fahrt*.

In the full tradition of the genre as it was in the 1930s the book has a map, mildly comical chapter titles ('The Bathroom Basin') as well as an introductory piece by the club's first president, G.K. Chesterton, full of the right paradoxical stuff such as 'We all talk of the mystery of Asia; and there is a sense in which we are all wrong'. Of the 13 contributors only two are names still ringing today, Christie, and Sayers, while others have receded more or less into the mists of time, Knox and Berkeley; Canon Victor White-church, author in 1912 of *Thrilling Stories of the Railway*; Henry Wade, the pen-name of Sir Henry Lancelot Aubrey-Fletcher, Bart., author of police procedural stories before that sub-genre had been thought of; Edgar Jepson, prolific writer of all sorts of fiction and father of the crime novelist, Selwyn Jepson; Clemence Dane, well known in her day as a playwright and author with Helen Simpson of two crime novels featuring an actor sleuth.

The book, which is still surprisingly readable, has as an appendix the solutions hoped for by most of the writers bar Anthony Berkeley to whom had fallen the hard task of, as his final chapter was called, 'Clearing Up the Mess'. In the good old tradition some of the explanations are nearly as lengthy as the mystery chapters themselves.

Not content with this success, the members of the club did it again in 1933. This time the book was based on a dilemma faced by Milward Kennedy. He had thought of a title, *Ask A Policeman*, from a music-hall song of the day, but was unable to think of a story to fit it.

He put his trouble to John Rhode, who wrote back, 'I have come to the conclusion that writing detective stories is just like any other vice. The deed is done without one's having any clear knowledge of the temptation that led up to it.' But he did supply a plot in the form of an opening chapter and then, adding complication to complication like good Detection Club members, four other writers each took one another's detectives and added four long chapters. Whereupon Milward Kennedy brought the whole to a conclusion. The four mid-field players were Gladys Mitchell, who changed sleuths with Helen Simpson, her Mrs Bradley 'the benign lizard' for Sir John Saumarez, actor manager; and Anthony Berkeley who swapped Roger Sheringham for Dorothy L. Sayers's Lord Peter.

In 1935 the odd art of round-robining sprang up in the United States when President Franklin Roosevelt, no less, told the author Fulton Oursler, who wrote crime as Anthony Abbot, that he had an

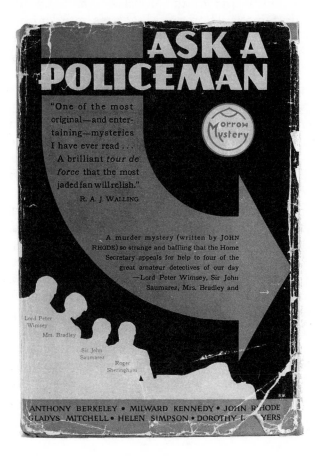

idea for a mystery. So 'the leading story writers' of the century were asked to turn idea into book. It is a thriller, of sorts, called *The President's Mystery Story*, and lacks much subtlety, perhaps because only Abbot himself, S.S. Van Dine and Samuel Hopkins Adams, were actual mystery writers among the various contributors.

As odd a venture in Britain was *Six Against the Yard* in 1936, in which six writers each wrote a 'perfect murder' story and then a former Scotland Yard man, George Cornish, pointed out where they had gone wrong. The six were Sayers, Berkeley, Crofts and Knox, stalwarts of the game by now, with Margery Allingham and Russell Thorndike, a member of the famed acting family.

In 1939 Sayers and Crofts returned unbloodied (except fictionally) to the fray with a serial commissioned by a newspaper, *Night of Secrets* (called *Double Death* as a book). To the old hands now were added F. Tennyson Jesse, editor of several of the *Notable British Trials* series and author of the novel *A Pin to See the Peepshow*, based on the famous Thompson-Bywaters murder case; Anthony Armstrong, humorist, playwright and occasional detective novelist; Valentine Williams, thriller writer creator of 'Clubfoot', and David Hume, a very prolific author, now largely forgotten, who suggested that the authors' notes might be added to the book. This was done at the end of each chapter, and has its fascination.

After World War II the many-hands notion struck in America once more when a dozen members of the California chapter of the Mystery Writers of America banded together as 'Theo Durrant' and produced *The Marble Forest* in 1951. Darwin Teilhet wrote only the three words of the title. Leonore Glen Offord, Anthony Boucher, Richard Shattuck, Eunice May Boyd, Florence Ostern Faulkner, Allen Hymson, Cary Lucas, Dana Lyon, Virginia Rath and William Worley contributed at greater length. Re-titled (poor Teilhet) *The Big Fear*, the book came out in paperback a couple of years later.

In 1953 the Britons took up the running again with *No Flowers By Request*, once again with Dorothy L. Sayers leading the way. Her collaborators here, in what set out as another newspaper serial, were Gladys Mitchell, Anthony Gilbert, (creator of Arthur Crook, ebullient solicitor); E.C.R. Lorac, like Gilbert a woman hiding behind a pseudonym and a prolific whodunitist; and Christianna Brand, who needed all her tremendous ingenuity to produce a concluding episode. Next year a different team, John Dickson Carr with Joan Fleming, Elizabeth Ferrars, (in Britain appearing without the meaningless middle initial X), and Laurence Meynell, later to produce a run of lightly amusing Hooky Heffernan tales, plus Valerie White and Michael Cronin neither now remembered, produced a fine romp, *Crime on the Coast*. All the British books have been re-published in recent years and are worth looking for if only as curiosities.

With the end of the 1950s the fun faded. But in 1979 the Detection Club was in financial low water once again and its then President, Julian Symons, proposed we put matters right in a version of the time-honoured way. No great games, however, now.

Instead, 13 of us undertook each to produce a story with a verdict in it, the whole to be titled (guess) *Verdict of Thirteen*. And, as of yore, it became something of a point of honour not to make one's verdict a simple jury one. So Peter Dickinson set his tale on the planet David, Michael Underwood set his at St Oswald's School, Patricia Highsmith took care the police would never know, and I myself made my jury the servants of a club in the India of the Raj who misunderstand almost everything they hear about the white sahibs but know all the same who done it.

Scribble, Scribble, Mr Gribble

Some authors have written an extraordinary number of crime books. Take Leonard Gribble. He is not one of the mystery greats. Indeed, Melvyn Barnes, author of *Murder in Print*, has nicely said of him that his almost total lack of characterisation makes his books 'a little less readable than one would wish'. But what he perhaps lacks in readability he made up for in productivity.

Starting in 1939 with *The Case of the Marsden Rubies*, he went on to give us a total of 45 crime novels ending in 1983 with – significant difference in style of title – *The Dead Don't Scream*. But that was not all. He was also Leo Grex, author of 26 crime stories, and Dexter Muir, who contributed a mere three. But then Mr Gribble was an adventure novelist, too, with another three titles under his own name, plus ten Westerns as Landon Grant and four as Lee Denver. Then add a volume of verse, *Toy Folk and Nursery People* and 66 non-fiction books, mostly in the true crime genre, and you have a pretty massive output.

However, there are plenty of other crime writers every bit as prolific. Take W. Murdoch Duncan, a Scot, who though he was born in 1909 did not start writing until 1944. But then, until his death in 1976, he made up for his long silence. With six other names on the go he produced a grand total of 219 titles (unless I've mis-counted).

He is rivalled by a rather better author, Erle Stanley Gardner, creator of Perry Mason, with 99 novels under his own name and 29 as A.A. Fair, creator of the vast, irascible, pecan waffle-fuelled Berta Cool and her diminutive sidekick Donald Lam. Reputedly he once wrote one of the books inside four days. In sheer numbers he may have been only half the weight of W. Murdoch Duncan (that Scottishly placed W, by the way, stands for simple William), but he ended up as a Mystery Writers of America Grand Master. And deservedly, for the steady pleasure his fiction, formula though it was, gave to countless readers over a stretch of 40 years. After all, the same again but a little different is what the great majority of us crime readers want.

It was what, too, was provided by another of the great prolificoes, if perhaps with rather more 'little difference' than Erle Stanley Gardner. Edgar Wallace produced books in half a dozen different veins, though all of them have in common a cracking, fast-paced story that doesn't bother too much about mere logic or a credibility much deeper than can stand up to a whizz-through read. At one stage in Britain every fourth book sold was a Wallace. He clocked up, by my count, 89 crime books and hundreds of crime short stories, besides much, much else. And all under his own name.

The books under the name of Leslie Charteris and featuring 'The Saint' cannot all be safely allocated to the writer who began life in Singapore as Leslie Yin, half-Chinese, half-English, and who later legally adopted the Charteris, a name chosen because of his admiration for Colonel Francis Charteris, eighteenth-century rake, gambler and a founder of the notorious Hellfire Club. But some 30 books, often consisting of three short novels can safely be attributed to the original pen.

Charteris began his writing career in England and had The Saint as a typical post-World War I ex-officer and social buccaneer, much

Leslie Charteris, the magazine that was
revived to celebrate his hero and (above) an
illustration from *Popular Detective* for 'The
Saints No Angel', 1938.

like the Bulldog Drummond of 'Sapper' if considerably more charming. Later he went to live in the United States and transferred the whole saga to an American setting. Finally he retired to England again and became something of a recluse.

Indeed, many people believed him dead, a fate that is apt to happen to crime writers. Peter Lovesey once received a letter that went

> I have read two or three of your detective stories about Sergeant Cribb with immense pleasure, but I have not written to thank you because I assumed you died many years ago. My husband says he thinks you may still be alive. We have quite an argument about it last night. I suppose it does not really matter, but we would be most grateful to have the question cleared up.

Imagine my own sense of awe, then, when in 1984 I was invited to lunch at a London hotel by John Ball, the author of *In the Heat of the Night* and other books about the black detective Virgil Tibbs, to meet Mr Charteris in person and discuss the revival of *The Saint Magazine* (alas, short-lived). I found the legendary author, who was born in 1907, sprightly as a 20-year-old and still paying homage in his life style to his old hero of Hellfire Club fame.

If Leslie Charteris, though a delightfully fizzy writer, was something of a formula fellow like Erle Stanley Gardner, that does not necessarily mean that all prolific authors have to abandon individuality. Think of Rex Stout, writing in America at much the same time as Gardner but contriving to be much less dependent on a formula even though the majority of his books featured the almost impossibly fat Nero Wolfe resolutely remaining inside his brown-

Rex Stout.   Simenon.

A *mélange* of Maigrets gathered together for the unveiling of Peter Dhondt's statue of Maigret in Delfzijl, Holland.

stone, invariably pressuring poor Archie Goodwin to do the legwork. Yet among them there are considerable variations.

Although Stout produced only 54 titles (only!), he did not begin as a crime novelist till 1934 when he was 41 himself and he 'retired' to devote himself to long-term fiction. In the years between 1912 and 1916 he had written reams of magazine fiction, and in old age he was able to boast of being 'the only professional writer who hasn't got a single unpublished paragraph in a drawer anywhere'. As a reader, too, he has, according to what he has told us, some astonishing records. He had read the Bible twice through by the age of three and had devoured his father's library of 1,200 books by the time he was ten.

To the tally of fine writers who were also extraordinarily productive one must add, of course, the name of Georges Simenon. He wrote more than 400 books in total and some 1,500 short stories, about half of the novels under his own name. In his early days, when he was really churning the stuff out, he used as many as 16 pseudonyms.

He wrote extraordinarily fast always. In his diary you can read: 'Saturday, June 3, 1961 . . . Terrible panic. I would like to begin a novel this afternoon . . . The last ten days I have lived with my characters.' And then: 'Saturday, June 10. 9.30 in the morning. Novel finished. I re-enter life.' But, far from being slapdash affairs, Simenon's work at this period of his life, whether featuring his Maigret or one of his 'hard' novels, is as fine crime fiction as there has ever been.

The Final Accolade

The palm for productivity in crime fiction, if not for literary excellence, should surely go to John Creasey, a fact granted a sort of official recognition when the sub-head for his obituary in 1973 in *The Times*, then most prestigious of papers, was 'A prolific thriller writer'. It was the final accolade in the productivity stakes.

John Creasey's total output in all forms of fiction has been calculated as exceeding 600 titles. But to those must be added the 700 rejection slips he received, and kept, before in 1932 he achieved publication for the first time.

He achieved this phenomenal output by using as many as 28 pseudonyms, of which J.J. Marric under which he produced what is probably his best work, the series of books about Gideon of Scotland Yard, is the best known. But he was also Elise Fecamps and Henry St John Cooper, romantic novelists both, and as Tex Riley he wrote in his earlier days Westerns. He once charmingly said that these went all right, once he had learnt to take the coyotes out of the sky.

In crime, a journalist once calculated, he wrote 560 novels in 40 years, a book every 26 days, or 56,000,000 words in total. His series figuring 'The Toff', a variant on 'The Saint', alone ran to 55 titles. It is an open secret, however, that in his latter years he employed 'checkers' to iron out the errors that inevitably crept in when producing at such a pace. But in principle he wrote every word that came under his name – that is, his 28 names.

Never Mind the Great Detectives . . .

What about the Great Crooks? Crime fiction is awash with Great Detectives, but it has not done too badly in the opposite department either. So let's see a score of them, arranged alphabetically since it would take a Dante (translated, of course, by Dorothy L. Sayers) to assign each to the proper circle of Hell.

1. Fantomas

Immensely popular in France from 1910 on (the last story about him appeared in 1963), he was the joint creation of Marcel Allain and Pierre Souvestre, a pair of journalists who came together over a shared delight in high-performance cars and founded a magazine for fellow fans called *Poids-Lourds*. They wrote the Fantomas books (until Souvestre died) in the same manner as the ladies called Emma Lathen, that is in alternate chapters. Their early runaway success brought them in a great deal of money. Fantomas is a malevolent genius who uses for his own ends all the resources of science and technology in an unending quest for wealth and power. A master of disguise (natch), his evil hand is never stayed by pity, never trembles in fear. So, of course, he was dubbed The Lord of Terror and, with typical French intellectualism, 'a modern Mephistopheles'. His wild adventures are beginning to come to paperback readers in English on both sides of the Atlantic.

2. Flambeau

That alone seems to have been his name. He was a worthy antagonist for G.K. Chesterton's Father Brown, being as different as could be from the dumpy, commonsensical little priest: 'a Gascon of gigantic stature and bodily daring' who on one occasion ran down the Rue de Rivoli with a policeman under each arm. 'His real crimes,' we are told, 'were chiefly those of ingenious and wholesale robbery. But each of his thefts was almost a new sin.' Of course, he was a master of disguise, and the head of the Paris police was ready to arrest on the spot 'a tall apple-woman, a tall grenadier, or even a tolerably tall duchess' though it fell, naturally, to Father Brown to be too much for him in the end. Sadly, he then degenerated into a sort of Archie Goodwin to that dumpy Great Detective's Nero Wolfe.

3. Fosco, Count

He is perhaps the most delightful of all the gallery of rogues (and goodies) created by that splendid writer, Wilkie Collins and too-little known for the most part. The machinator behind the mysterious goings-on of *The Woman in White*, Collins said once that he had to

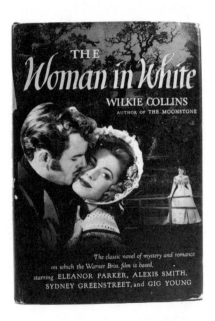

make Fosco a foreigner because his crime was 'too ingenious' for an English villain, by which I hazard he meant too ingenious for an English readership to believe an Englishman could rise to. Collins always had his audience well under control. 'Make 'em laugh, make 'em weep, make 'em wait' was his rule. And in Fosco he makes us laugh first, at the fearful fatness of the man, at the pet mice he lets frisk over his waistcoat, at his feminine light-footedness. Then the sinisterness and the steeliness beneath strike home and, if perhaps we don't quite weep, we certainly wait with baited breath for his next move. No wonder Prime Minister Gladstone put off a theatre party so as to be able to finish the book and find Fosco foiled.

4. *Godahl, the Infallible*

The creation, in 1914, of Frederick Irving Anderson, Godahl has been described by that indefatigable commentator on things criminal, Otto Penzler, as 'the greatest of all American crooks'. As his name implies, he was so good at being bad that he was never even suspected of his crimes. E.F. Bleiler, the authority on Victorian and supernatural fiction, has said of Anderson's stories that they have a 'Stevensonian glamour and fairytale quality' as well as being 'intelligent, original, well-crafted, excellent in characterisation, and often brilliant stylistically'. What more could one ask?

5. *Gutman, Caspar*

He was villain enough to task Sam Spade to the full in Dashiell Hammett's seminal *The Maltese Falcon*. 'Let me have men about me who are fat,' Shakespeare made Julius Caesar beg. He might well have been asking for a good crime-story villain. 'The fat man was flabbily fat with bulbous pink cheeks and lips and chins and neck, with a great soft egg of a belly,' Hammett wrote. But Gutman has, too, an oily resilience that goes counter to what might be purely disgusting in him. 'By Gad, sir,' he frequently exclaims in admiration of Sam Spade's toughness, and you feel that he is a worthy adversary.

6. *Lone Wolf, The*

Louis Joseph Vance, the American writer of short stories by the hundred who died in 1933, brought the Lone Wolf to life in a book of that name published in 1914, or, you could say, he was brought yet more to life in a film (of that name) made as early as 1917 and in a string of others that followed. But film Lone Wolf was always on the side of the angels, even if he played a bit dirty. Book Lone Wolf (it has been claimed he gave the expression to the language) was a badder baddie. His regal name was Michael Lanyard but – first piece of wickedness – he was brought up as Michael Troyon, drudge-of-all-work in a disreputable Paris hotel, and if such a hotel is in Paris you can bet it's good and disreputable. Michael was forced to lie and to steal and even to cheat until he tried to pinch something from a top-notch thief by the name of Bourke (aristocratic, you can tell) but, darkly handsome youth that he was, instead of getting his come-uppance he became Bourke's pupil and rose up to be a master criminal in his own right, respected and sophisticated by day and a daring thief by night. In his first adventure a band of underworld nasties threatened to reveal his secret unless he joined their pack. Hence, on his scornful refusal, the soubriquet. But, of course, of course, even book Lone Wolf falls in love and becomes such a goody eventually that he works for the British Secret Service and foils an attempt to assassinate the King. Hip, hip, hooray.

7. *Lovejoy*

By this name alone the hero of Jonathan Gash's lively books with an antiques background is known. And as a buyer of antiques, and one not above a little forging of them, Lovejoy must rank, hero though he be, as a great crook. He's always getting ladies into bed, too, which must be a naughty thing to do. Witness what that scholarly organ *The Times Literary Supplement* has said of him: 'Spouting antiques lore by the yard and getting off with anyone wearing a skirt who comes within pouncing distance.' He can murder a worse guy than himself with a fine ruthlessness, though generally he finds a sharply witty crack to sugar the pill. But villain he is, nevertheless. Look at the very last words of his foray into Ireland, *The Sleepers of Erin*: 'I slammed the door and walked out whistling, heartbreak forgotten.'

8. Lugg, Magersfontein

Valet to Mr Albert Campion in the marvellously romantic novels of Margery Allingham, and former convict not above wanting to return to moderately wicked ways in the service of the good. He deals with the ups and downs of life with magnificent crudity. 'Not 'arf a funny bloke outside,' he whispered hoarsely once. 'A foreigner. Shall I chuck a brick at 'im?' A hillock of a man 'with a big pallid face which reminded one irresistibly of a bull terrier', he is practically bald, but, says his creator, 'by far the most outstanding thing about him was the all-pervading impression of melancholy he conveyed'. Born, doubtless, in 1899, year of the Boer War battle of Magersfontein, he will surely live as long as crime books are read.

9. Lupin, Arsène

Gentleman-cambrioleur, as Maurice Leblanc labelled him on his first appearance in 1907. The description pretty well says it all, provided you know that a *cambrioleur* is a burglar. But he does on occasion do worse than burgle. Towards the end of *813*, for instance, we read of his three murders, followed, be it said, by his remorseful suicide.

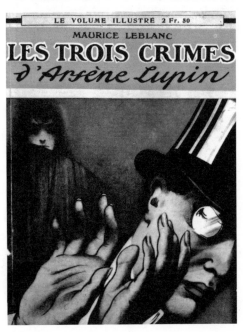

Only, at the last moment he thinks it better to be alive. He also had the impertinence to run rings round an English detective with a strong resemblance to Sherlock Holmes. Finally, he was a great favourite with the boy Jean-Paul Sartre. 'I adored the Cyrano of the underworld,' he wrote, looking back from his eminence as a philosopher, 'without realising that he owed his herculean strength, his sharp courage, his typically French intelligence to our being caught trouserless in 1870.' A 'typically French' view of the disastrous Franco-Prussian War, one might add.

10. *Manchu, Dr Fu*

Sax Rohmer, Fu Manchu's originator, told in a radio talk in 1934 how, prowling London's Limehouse district in the early years of the century, 'one night, and appropriately enough it was a foggy night, I saw a tall and very dignified Chinaman alight from a car. He was accompanied by an Arab girl, or she may have been Egyptian, and as I saw the pair enter a mean-looking house, and as the fog drew a curtain over the scene, I conceived the character of Dr Fu Manchu.' Rohmer was a terrible romancer, but the story of the birth of the evil oriental who attempted time and again to achieve world domination will do nicely. Like many another villain, alas, Fu Manchu came to a sticky end, a stickily sentimental end: he joined forces with the West to defeat imperialistic communism.

11. *Mannering, John, also known as The Baron*

One of the many, many creations of John Creasey, writing as Anthony Morton when the stories first appeared with *Meet the Baron* or in America *The Man in the Blue Mask* in 1937. This was written in six days flat and entered for a competition for a book featuring a 'cracksman' with a hefty prize at that time of £1,500. It scooped the pool. Forty-nine books later, in 1979, came the end of the Baron's career as a man-about-town jewel thief, soon reformed. Why will decent baddies so often go to the good? Generally, I'm afraid to say, it's because they marry someone like 'the lovely Lorna Fauntley'.

Randolph Mason depicted by William Dixon.

12. *Mason, Randolph*

A lawyer, he was the creation in 1896, before the coming of the mightily good Uncle Abner, of Melville Davisson Post. Skilful and unscrupulous, Randolph Mason used the law to defeat the ends of justice, getting criminals off the hook by finding them (if this isn't a mixed metaphor) legal loopholes. His creator justified him by saying that 'nothing but good could come out of exposing the law's defects' and, as a result of some of this tales, the laws of the land were actually changed. Wicked Mason's final book appearance was called *The Corrector of Destinies*, a description to be applied, ironically enough, many years later by Simenon to his Maigret, that soul of goodness. Erle Stanley Gardner's Perry Mason was named after him.

13. Moriarty, Professor James

Conan Doyle dubbed him the Napoleon of Crime, and subsequent commentators have seen him as the Nietzschean superman incarnated. He was 'a man of good birth', – important that – 'and excellent education, endowed by nature with a phenomenal mathematical faculty' (such, indeed, that one of the fictional papers attributed to him actually anticipated in its title one of Einstein's). But 'a criminal strain ran in his blood' and he set out to dominate in secret the world of London evil-doing, only to be foiled in the series of encounters with Sherlock Holmes that ended in a reversible death plunge over the Reichenbach Falls. A plunge reversed in Moriarty's case, not by Doyle, but by the eminent pasticheur of James Bond, John Gardner. Professor Moriarty also possessed the singularly wicked attribute of having two brothers called James. One, we learnt in *The Valley of Fear*, was a stationmaster in the West of England; the other, Colonel James Moriarty, wrote letters to *The Times*, we were told in 'The Final Problem', vindicating his brother's life. They were, Dr Watson assured us, an absolute perversion of the facts (though I suppose, if any facts were perverted, careless old Doyle was the criminal).

14. Peterson, Carl

The opponent 'Sapper' found for his Bulldog Drummond. A wicked foreigner, he took his 'sound old English name' as part of his general fiendishness, though he was not cunning enough to alter the 'Carl'. He is set against Drummond's utter Englishness, as exemplified by his use of the boot on 'the poorer type of clerk . . . that screams insults at a football referee' and by his use of the cat on 'Hebrews'. Peterson is – what else could he be? – a master of disguise. On one occasion even he thinned out his hair with a razor, sacrifice of vanity, in order to become Mr William Robinson, owner of a house on the border of the New Forest, and then, yet more masterly, he instantly grew the hair back again to resume a former disguise as Mr Edward Blackton. But who was he really under all those disguises? We shall never know. When at the end of the fourth book about him, *The Final Count*, he is at last dealt with, we read: 'For full five seconds did he stand there before the end came. And in that five seconds the mask slipped from his face, and he stood revealed for what he was. And of that revelation no man can write.'

15. Raffles, A.J.

E.W. Hornung's amateur cracksman, amateur cricketer, 'a dangerous bat, a brilliant field, and perhaps the very finest slow bowler of his decade', his decade being the magical 1890s. Raffles was above all a gentleman (which, as George Orwell pointed out, was better than being a nobleman), but he was a classy gentleman all right. He had rooms in Albany, exclusive block off Piccadilly, arranged 'with the right amount of negligence and the right amount of taste'. He smoked only Sullivans, smartest of cigarettes. His manners were faultless. His consideration for others (unless he was robbing them) never faltered. He quoted Keats. He roused such admiration in Bunny Manders, who had been his fag at school, that Bunny followed him, nervous but loyal, on the most daring of his exploits. He died, heroically of course, fighting for Queen and Country in

South Africa. His creator's obituary for him was: 'Raffles was a villain when all was written; it is of no service to his memory to gloze the fact.' Certainly the editor of the New York scandal magazine *Town Topics* in 1904 was not inclined to 'gloze' Raffles's villainy. He concluded an attack on one Pat Collier, owner of a rival publication, as being 'lecherous, leprous and unable to write his name' by accusing him of debauching the youth of America in serialising the adventures of the amateur cracksman.

16. *Ripley, Tom*

Patricia Highsmith might have written an obituary for her Tom Ripley similar to E.W. Hornung's for his Raffles. There is no glozing the fact that Tom is a villain, a murderer indeed. He has appeared in four novels and in book after book somebody dies at his hands. Yet . . . Yet he is a hero, at least for many of us, though I can remember a meeting of the judges for the Gold Dagger award at which the distinguished critic, the late Marghanita Laski, vowed to resign if we gave the prize to such an immoral book. But Tom has tremendous charm, and, more, he truly loves his beautiful French wife, Hélène, and the lovely garden that came to him with her and which he works in with warm pleasure. And he tells us, too, about the world we live in. The man he will murder, in *Ripley Under Ground* exclaims in exasperation, 'I cannot understand your total disconnection with the truth of things.' But Tom exists to tell us that such simplicities are no more. We live in a fluid world, and he shows us how we can bear to.

17. *Simpson, Arthur Abdel*

I think he is the most engaging baddie I have ever encountered, in real life or in the pages. I met him first in Eric Ambler's 1962 book *The Light of Day* and felt myself lucky to encounter him again in 1967 in *Dirty Story*. His very first words showed him for what he was, a double-dealer, but somehow sympathetic with it: 'It came down to this: if I had not been arrested by the Turkish police, I would have been arrested by the Greek police.' Son of a British commissioned sergeant-major and an Egyptian woman, he contrives to get an education in England that lets him pass as a 'gentleman'. His only inheritance otherwise is two paternal precepts: 'Never volunteer' and 'Bullshit baffles brains'. Some of the questions he asks us are: 'Is it a crime to earn money?' (even by poncing) and 'Why shouldn't people be told what they want to hear?' (blatant lies). He is a great one for wriggling out of things. At school it was rugby football ('childish, smelly, homosexual horseplay') and when caught stealing he is completely ready to burst into tears if this will help. He even gets out of it in the end when he has assisted at a monster robbery from the Topkapi Museum in Istanbul. And, he says, 'I have only really been arrested ten or twelve times in my whole life.'

18. Teatime, Miss Lucilla

She is the altogether engaging con-lady invented by the late Colin Watson in his chronicles of that sex-ridden and subversive town of Flaxborough. For her age, which is uncertain, she is remarkably trim and handsome. 'People instinctively approved of her, for there was in her appearance the flattering suggestion that she had taken pains to spare one personally the spectacle of yet another dumpy, disgruntled, defeated old woman.' When she asks, in a ladylike manner, for 'a little whisky' she hopes for and generally gets a double. And she is tough. Threatened with death, she discourages the man with the gun by pointing out to him that 'already there has crept into that incommodious mind of yours the realisation that I should never have been fool enough to come here without taking some precaution' and a little later when the murderer's wife yells, 'Where's my husband?' Miss Teatime, con-lady supreme, replies regretfully, 'I'm afraid he's in that cesspool thing down the garden.'

19. Templar, Simon, otherwise the Saint

Leslie Charteris made him and at first he made him bad. Later, as is the way, he became good. His rather engaging creed was that danger is good for you. (It's particularly engaging, I myself find, if the danger is safely stuck on the printed pages.) You feel more intensely alive, the Saint believed, when danger threatens. So he broke the law, and despised the police as 'excellent fellows for keeping an eye on pedestrian crossings and closing down night clubs and preventing people having a drink at the wrong time . . . and generally adding to the perpetual hilarity of English life'. Words taken from a radio talk by Charteris as long ago as 1934. The Saint, his creator added, wanted more than that, such as 'a complete callousness about blipping the ungodly over the beezer'. But it is the ungodly he blips, note. Already there were signs of the goody-goodness creeping in.

20. Velvet, Nick

Exclusively a great crook in short stories, written by the king of crime shorts (anything up to 700 under his belt) Ed Hoch, though there are two book-length collections of Velvet exploits. He is a thief *extraordinaire*, stealing with splendid ingenuity only very odd items of no value, for a minimum fee of $20,000, upped to $30,000 for specially dangerous assignments. Among his coups have been the theft of an entire baseball team, of the water from a swimming pool, of a sea serpent, of a vacuum. His dear wife, Gloria, believes he works for the Government, and does not lose her naïve trust in him even when she overhears him pretending to be a reporter, satisfied at once with the assurance that article writing is something 'I might take up'. After a dozen years of living with him, we are told, 'she was used to his odd behaviour'.

8 KINDS OF
CRIMINOSITY

Hermetically Sealed

What is the room you leave without entering, and what is room you enter without leaving? Old riddle. And the answers are: the womb and the tomb.

Like many ancient riddles, saws and fairy tales apparently absurdly simple yet continuing to exert a sway over generation after generation, this double conundrum pings off an echo from something deep in the psyche. And it is from this deeper, hidden meaning that those mysteries classed as locked-room stories gain their uncanny hold. There can be no more securely locked room than the tomb into which we all must go, figuratively at least; there can be no greater mystery than the mystery of death.

So from the earliest days of crime fiction there have been written and obsessively read what John Dickson Carr, master of this subgenre, loved to call stories of the hermetically sealed chamber, inside which a body is found but no murderer and often no murder weapon. (Hint: freeze some water in a dagger-shaped mould, as first dreamt up, I think, by Edgar Jepson and Robert Eustace in a *Strand Magazine* story, 'The Tea-Leaf'.)

Indeed, if mystery fiction began with Edgar Allan Poe, as in effect it did, then it began with a tale in *Graham's Magazine* for April 1841, the locked-room story 'The Murders in the Rue Morgue', in which the mysterious deaths occur in a room elaborately described as being impenetrable to any human being.

Poe clearly in producing his piece of ingenuity had his eye on higher things. He wanted in creating the mystery solver, the Chevalier Dupin, creature of the night, to put before the world a

Bela Lugosi in a film version of Poe's story 'Murder in the Rue Morgue' with Leon Waycoff.

new romantic hero capable of breaking old classical bonds. His followers, increasingly, have concentrated simply on the ingenuity. But behind whatever contrivances they have dreamt up still lies that old riddle, simple yet profoundly affecting, What is the room you enter without leaving?

There is still a good deal of the ultimate mystery of things echoing, however, in Conan Doyle's 'The Adventure of the Speckled Band' with its hints of exotic gipsies, its serpent of old, and that client's response to being asked what makes her shiver, 'It is fear, Mr Holmes. It is terror.' In it, too, you get the classic description of the hermetically sealed chamber:

> The door had been fastened upon the inner side, and the windows were blocked by old-fashioned shutters with broad iron bars, which were secured every night. The walls were carefully sounded and were shown to be quite solid all round, and the flooring was also thoroughly examined, with the same result. The chimney is wide, but it is barred up by four large staples. It is certain, therefore, that my sister was quite alone when she met her end.

But in the same year as the book publication of that story in the short novel *The Big Bow Mystery* by Israel Zangwill, written at the invitation of the *Star* newspaper, mere ingenuity, though ingenuity of a high order, is to the fore in the recounting of the 'murder of a man in a room to which there was no possible access' in the Bow district of London. Some 15 years later, in France, there followed Gaston Leroux's novel *The Mystery of the Yellow Chamber* (recalled by Agatha Christie in her search for the detective who became Hercule Poirot), a book that John Dickson Carr proclaimed as 'the best detective tale ever written'.

Israel Zangwill.

Other locked-room tales of equal ingenuity, and plenty of less, followed hot-foot. Melville Davisson Post produced his Uncle Abner story 'The Doomdorf Mystery', one of the best and one with plenty of deep-sounding echo to it as well. In 1927 S.S. Van Dine produced another classic of the art with *The Canary Murder Case*, in which (to give things away a little) a piece of twisted wire plays a key part, as it punningly had in Edgar Wallace's *The Clue of the New Pin* in 1923, perhaps less magisterially. In 1934 there was another classic, Ellery Queen's *The Chinese Orange Mystery*, the reading of which 'perched in a tree in a gully behind my house' set the pre-teenager who was to become Donald A. Yates, Professor of Spanish American Literature,

UNDERWOOD AND UNDERHAND

There must be something about the name Underwood that has a special affinity for crime writing. First, there is the crime writer Michael Underwood, the pseudonym adopted by Michael Evelyn when he began his now long series of crime novels set in legal circles and was still a senior official in the office of the Director of Public Prosecutions. His most intriguing title is surely *A Trout in the Milk*, a quotation from the great American man of letters, Thoreau: 'Some circumstantial evidence is very strong, as when you find a trout in the milk.'

What then do we deduce has been secretly added when we find an Underwood in the crime story? In that classic 'impossible crime' tale by Selwyn Jepson and Robert Eustace 'The Tea-leaf', we discover 'a fussy old gentleman by the name of Underwood', while in another story first seen in the *Strand Magazine*, sacred repository of Sherlockery, 'Primrose Petals' by H.C. Bailey, now too neglected author of the Reggie Fortune detective novels, who appears but 'the faithful Underwood' of the County Police.

Finally (or as finally as my researches go), in Freeman Wills Crofts' detective story *Fear Comes to Chalfont* we have 'a clerk named Underwood who has been arrested for theft'.

off on a side-career as a writer of 'impossible crime' stories and historian of the sub-genre.

And on they went. High among them the many contributions of John Dickson Carr and his *alter ego* Carter Dickson, including Chapter 17 in the book which a panel of crime critics once voted as clearly the best of all locked-room novels, *The Three Coffins* (yes, for Britons *The Hollow Man*) entitled 'The Locked-room Lecture' ('We're in a detective story, and we don't fool the reader by pretending we're not . . . Let us candidly glory in the noblest pursuit possible to characters in a book.').

Add, too, the contributions of Carr's great rival, less known in Britain, Clayton Rawson, creator of Merlini the magician, in the

1930s and 1940s. In answer to a challenge from Rawson, Carr, or rather Carter Dickson, produced one of his most cunning attempts in 1944, *He Didn't Kill Patience*. Add again the ingenuities of Dorothy L. Sayers and G.K. Chesterton in short stories, and on once more to that very short, very ingenious 'locked pier' mystery 'As If By Magic' of Julian Symons, together with some of those of Edmund Crispin. And even those rather serious sociological Swedes, Maj Sjowall and Per Wahloo, produced a book in 1973 called simply *The Locked Room*, while the equally serious, in a different way, Simenon, had a single short story in the mode, 'The Little House at Croix-Rouge' published in a French magazine in 1927.

Or, for that matter, why don't I put in a rather less ingenious but desperately classical variation on the theme, *Go West, Inspector Ghote*? For that I adapted a real-life attempt by a vengeful suicide to create a death in an hermetically sealed place which I had heard tell of at a lecture by a forensic scientist in California. Only, in dull old reality the police investigators quite quickly found that chamber not so hermetically sealed. But that's life. In art it took Inspector Ghote quite some while to hit on the secret.

Maj Sjöwall and Per Wahlöö.

Schools for Skulduggery

I suppose the extra fascination of murder stories set in schools is in the presence of what may be seen as the ultimate evil amid what may be seen as utter innocence. Of course, the murder of one individual, even a schoolboy, can be outdone as evil by all sorts of horrors, and, equally, schoolboys and even schoolgirls are not precisely without their flicks of the bad in human nature.

I seized on this myself a many years ago when *Ellery Queen's Mystery Magazine* (for ever to be praised) ran a competition, confined with splendid American generosity to British writers, for a new crime short story. I set my entry in an English preparatory school, such as I had spent some of the least happy days of my life in, and one of which my father had owned. I balked, however, at having a human being, even a boy, murdered and made my corpse a pet robin, thus enabling me to called my story, which won second prize, 'Who Killed Cock Robin?'

Dear, twinkling Fred Dannay, the other half of 'Ellery Queen' with his cousin, Manfred Lee, who always changed a title if he could, asked me for a different one and when the story appeared in the magazine and subsequent anthologies it was called 'The Justice Boy', the justice boy in question being the 'detective' named, of course, Watson. He had no first name. In the days in which I set my story, the 1930s, first names were shame-making secrets in school.

All of which is preliminary to looking at some murder stories set in that specially attractive background, the school. Attractive, one is bound to add, much more to British writers than to American. There are plenty of American mysteries set in colleges, notably Helen Eustis's splendid novel, *The Horizontal Man*. But, perhaps because there are fewer enclosed boarding schools in the United States, I can call to mind only a very few school-set American mysteries. Back in the 1930s Stuart Palmer's popular sleuth, Miss Hildegarde Withers, was, of course, a retired teacher (the smell of chalk clung to her for years afterwards) and once she did investigate a case, *Murder on the Blackboard*, in her own school. Recently perhaps murder in and around the classroom does seem to be rearing its head, in such a book as Joan Hess's *Dear Miss Demeanour* of 1986 set in a high school where both the janitor and the principal meet sticky ends.

However, the closed society of the traditional boarding school in England has provided a fine crop from British writers, though I cannot claim to know every one of them. The earliest I am aware of came in 1933. It was called simply *Murder at School*, though when published in America it became *Was It Murder?* Originally it was said to be by 'Glen Trevor', but this was in fact James Hilton, author of such bestsellers as *Lost Horizon* and *Random Harvest* as well as that schmaltzy novel of school life, *Goodbye, Mr Chips*. In *Murder at School* a boy is the victim, the school is called Oakington and, very 1930s, there is much debate about whether it ranks as a 'pukka' public school or is merely a fee-paying, slightly lower-class establishment. The jacket artist for the US paperback in 1980 had no doubts: he drew a small boy in top hat and Eton collar.

In 1935 there came a first detective story, *A Question of Proof*, by a then heavily anonymous author 'Nicholas Blake', set in a prep school, very well observed in both staff room and playing fields. The school toady, the Hon. Algernon Wemyss-Wyvern (that's going it a bit), and the obnoxious headmaster both get done. Before long, of course, it leaked out that Blake was the then 'modern' poet, Cecil Day Lewis, and that his detective, Nigel Strangeways, was based on his fellow shocking poet, W.H. Auden (who many years later in an essay 'The Guilty Vicarage' was to recommend a college as a properly enclosed group for the authentic detective story, and who yet later was to be the 'background' for Amanda Cross's donnish detection, *Poetic Justice*).

Day Lewis had done his stint of teaching at no fewer than three schools, and many of the other authors who have used a school setting wrote from experience, often bitter. But I would think that Michael Gilbert's memories of school are rosy. Perhaps at the Cathedral School in Salisbury, where he taught while studying to become a lawyer, he did not experience the full horror of the chalk-smelling, furniture-dilapidated dreariness of the typical staff room. Two of his novels have school settings, his first, in 1947, *Close Quarters*, and his 1976 book, *The Night of the Twelfth*, which contrasts with tremendous effectiveness the evil that can stalk the world (in this instance a couple who torture small boys to death) and the innocence that lies in youth. Its almost final words are 'If only you could do it . . . lock the gate. Shut out all the disturbing influences, and live for ever in an innocent cloud-cuckoo land among people who never grew up.'

A year after *Close Quarters* came the detective story in which Edmund Crispin took advantage of his years as a schoolmaster, *Love Lies Bleeding*, the first words of which are 'The Headmaster sighed.' Mostly about musicians, and great fun, it takes Crispin's zany Professor Fen to Castrevenford School and Castrevenford High School for Girls, whose formidable headmistress, Miss Parry (all the characters are named after church music composers), prefers American cigarettes as having 'fewer chemicals'.

A year later again there came Gladys Mitchell's *Tom Brown's Body* with its echo of that famous tale of Dr Arnold's Rugby, Thomas Hughes's *Tom Brown's Schooldays*. Miss Mitchell, who in her day taught English and History ending her career at Matthew Arnold (brother of the Rugby head) School, Staines, also used a school setting for part of her 1954 book, *Faintley Speaking*, which has been published in the US only as recently as 1986. Her *Death at the Opera*, of 1934, despite its title is also set in a school, a 'progressive' one. A progressive school, too, was the setting for Julian Symons' 1956 book, *The Paper Chase* (*Bogue's Fortune* in the US) in which a crime-writer takes a job there for 'copy' and, of course, meets real murder.

The year 1954 was a particularly good one for school murder with, as well, a novella, *Safer Than Love*, from Margery Allingham (it comes, with another, under the title *No Love Lost*) set in a school just as the long summer holiday is beginning ('The rose-red buildings looking forbidding and forlorn as schools do out of term time') with the headmaster's new wife finding her husband dead. And there was that year *The Odd Flamingo*, one of the two crime stories with which Nina Bawden began her distinguished career as a novelist. The title is hardly the name of a school; it is in fact that of a seedy club. But the main part of the book concerns another headmaster's wife, also neglected, who finds her husband accused of fathering a child on a young girl.

Headmasters are particularly useful to crime writers as blackmail victims, unwilling murderers or suspects. They are required to be as respectable as a clergyman but it is somehow more possible to see them as running to sexual peccadilloes. A recent example of the Head as ever liable to embarrassment out of which murder can arise is Robert Barnard's *At Death's Door*. To that one can add another recent book, described to me as 'brilliant', *The Killjoy* by Anne Fine.

Agatha Christie, always a sympathetic if never a sentimental observer of children, set just one of her many books in a school, *Cat*

Among Pigeons in 1959. Meadowbank is a school for girls based, it seems, on the school Mrs Christie's daughter, Rosalind, went to. Both the setting and the staff (who one by one are being murdered) are convincingly portrayed, if the mass of motives that Hercule Poirot reveals needs the customary suspension of disbelief. Little though I knew it at the time, I myself was to tread closely on the Christean heels with *A Rush on the Ultimate* in 1961. Though chiefly using a croquet setting (having 'a rush on the penultimate' is a croquet term) I placed this in an out-of-term time prep school very much like the one I went to at Bexhill-on-sea, Sussex, though with elements from the school my father owned. Once again it is the headmaster who is murdered, with a croquet mallet (what else?). The notion for the book, in fact, came to me with the atrocious pun 'with mallet aforethought' and at first it was going to be about do-it-yourself house repair. But my headmaster, a portrait of one I had been kept in order by, was much nicer than most other victims.

In the following year a writer who went on to very different things set his second book, a plain detective novel *A Murder of Quality*, in a public school somewhat resembling the Eton where he had taught. John le Carré's detective was a rather mysterious visitor by the name of Smiley, though the affair had no smack of spying about it. The boys hardly come in, though le Carré was to write with tremendous insight about schoolboys at the beginning of *Tinker, Tailor, Soldier, Spy* when the discredited agent, Prideaux, takes a job as a prep school master, as well as naming another book, *The Honourable Schoolboy*.

With the decade of the 1960s entering its middle period the crime books set in schools take on a new colour. No longer do they, by and large, feature the élite prep and public schools. Instead they take for their settings the ordinary state school. Such a one was D.M. Devine's *His Own Appointed Day* in 1965, a solidly descriptive book with characters who have understandable problems. Somewhat similar was a first novel in 1966, *A Taste of Power* by W.J. Burley, another teacher turned writer, much influenced by Simenon. He also wrote, in 1977, *The Schoolmaster*, a story convincingly told, of a sensitive man with a load of guilt. Yet another book in this vein is *Golden Rain* by Douglas Clark, published in 1980, a girls' school murder case.

Reverting somewhat to an earlier age in tone are the books written by Elizabeth Lemarchand after she had retired early from her post as headmistress, owing to illness. Her first in 1967, *Death of An Old*

Leo Bruce's schoolmaster sleuth also entered
the world of train murders.

Girl, takes place at a school reunion. So many of her subsequent
books had schools in them that the Commissioner once says to her
detective, Tom Pollard, that if he keeps on being involved in such
cases he will end up as a teacher himself. To these harking-back
books we can add *Upperdown*, Stephen Cook's 1985 book, set in a
posh boarding school but very different from those of old in that an
explosion reveals an unpopular housemaster as wearing baby-doll
pyjamas. And there is also Michael Underwood's 1979 *Victim of
Circumstances*.

Finally, let me add one more to the roll of teachers who have
turned to crime – as distinct from fictional schoolmaster turned
detective (such as Lee Bruce's Carolus Deane in *Death at St Asprey's*
and *Case With Rope and Rings*), – B.M. Gill was a teacher, though
later she became – a fascinating career change – a chiropodist. Her

first book, *Death Prop*, is an account of the reactions of a man whose son has apparently fallen to his death on a school outing. He finally gets the opportunity to mete out his own rough justice and has to decide how to use his power over another person's life. Almost the last words of the book are: 'He could look with some coolness at the school half-hidden in the belt of trees.'

Putting on the Mockers

Putting on the mockers is, in fact, an expression derived from the Yiddish *makeh*, a boil or furuncle (one of Frank Parrish's delightful Dan Mallett, poacher-detective, stories *Bait on the Hook* is translated in French as *La Chasse aux Furoncles*). The Englished Yiddish expression means 'to bring misfortune on someone or something', and that is not exactly what parodies and pastiches of crime stories do, though they mock a little. But both a pastiche, which is an imitation as exact as its author can make it, and a parody, which is an exaggeration of the characteristics of an author, are tributes to their originals and are hardly successful unless done with a generous admixture of love.

Of course, the most parodied and pastiched of all crime fiction are the stories of Sherlock Holmes. Just a year after the first of the short stories, in the *Strand Magazine* in 1891, there appeared in *The Idler* a series *The Adventures of Sherlaw Kombs* written by one 'Luke Sharp' (look sharp), otherwise Robert Barr, who was later to write, among much else, *The Triumphs of Eugene Valmont*, eight linked stories, a sort of pre-Poirot, about a French ex-police officer working privately in England. Valmont's most triumphant triumph was 'Lord Chizzlerigg's Missing Fortune'.

Other parodies of Holmes followed in a torrent down the years with such heroes as Hemlock Jones, Shylock Holmes, Picklock Holes, Shirley Holmes, Sheerluck Holmes, Schlock Holmes. Even James Joyce in *Finnegan's Wake* contributed at least the name

Shedlock Holmes, while other celebrated writers to join in were Mark Twain in 1902 with 'A Double-barelled Detective Story' which featured Fetlock Jones, nephew of you-know-who, – Twain's story 'Life on the Mississippi' of 1883, incidentally, was the first to use a thumb print as identification – and J.M. Barrie in 1924 with 'The Adventure of the Two Collaborators'. Doyle himself even wrote a miniature parody 'How Watson Learned the Trick' to enshrine in the dolls' house made in the 1920s for Queen Mary and still to be seen at Windsor.

The Holmes stories have been pastiched pretty well to death, too. Indeed, *Ellery Queen's Mystery Magazine,* that great receptacle and temple of all that is short or shortish in crime fiction, eventually decreed that they would print no more Holmes pieces, thereby losing to *John Creasey's Crime Collection 1983* my own contribution to the art, 'The Adventure of the Suffering Ruler' in which, again, Watson triumphs and Holmes gets it all wrong. I am not sure whether the novel where Holmes also cuts a poor figure, Nicholas Meyer's *The Seven Per Cent Solution* is pastiche or parody, but whichever it was it brought its author much success and movie money.

Among the more skilful Holmesean take-offs must be listed *The Exploits of Sherlock Holmes* which John Dickson Carr wrote with Arthur Conan Doyle's son, Adrian, in 1954 and a long series about an appropriately twin-syllable first name, single-syllable surnamed sleuth, Solar Pons, the work of August Derleth.

Derleth, who was born in Sauk City, Wisconsin, lived there and died there in 1971, was known in his day as 'a one-man fiction factory', producing more than 130 books and innumerable short stories, seven volumes of them featuring his Holmes look-alike, Solar Pons. Something of an infant prodigy as a writer, beginning at 13 and achieving publication at 15, in 1927 when he was 19 he wrote to Sir Arthur Conan Doyle to ask if there would ever be any more stories about his beloved Sherlock Holmes. He got a non-committal reply, and so set out to provide similar fare himself and created Pons. Vincent Starrett, the notable Holmes scholar and author of *The Private Life of Sherlock Holmes*, the first 'biography' of the great detective, as well as what has been hailed as the best pastiche of them all, 'The Unique Hamlet', said of Derleth's stories, 'Solar Pons is – as it were – an ectoplasmic emanation of his great prototype . . . a clever impersonator with a twinkle in his eye, which tells us he is not Sherlock Holmes, and knows that *we* know it, but he hopes that we will like him anyway.'

Lancelot Speed's 1892 illustration of Sherlaw Kombs with Dr Whatson in a ditch.

Allied to the Holmes pastiches and parodies there are the books written by John Gardner, himself a noted espionage writer and continuer of the James Bond saga, about Holmes's great antagonist in a pair of novels he called the *Moriarty Journals*. He has said of them that they were an attempt to recreate 'the arch enemy of the stuffy Sherlock Holmes' within a framework of a factual reconstruction of the Victorian criminal world. To these may be added Barry Perowne's pastiches of A.J. Raffles, the gentleman burglar invented by Conan Doyle's brother-in-law, E.W. Hornung, somewhat to Doyle's disapproval. Hornung dedicated his first Raffles volume to 'A.C.D. This sincerest form of flattery'.

Perowne's stories ran on from 1933 to 1979, so they can hardly be called unsuccessful. Yet to my mind, I must confess, they are not quite all they should be, perhaps because Perowne makes his Raffles more of a goody than Hornung's fine creation. Hornung's original stole for the thrill of it: Perowne's imitation has become a sort of Robin Hood, doing good by stealthy burglarious entry. Perhaps the words of the great Dr Arnold of Rugby School should be borne in mind here, when he advised his pupils not to read imitations 'as they suggest themselves to the mind for ever after in connection with the beautiful pieces which they parody'.

An author whom one does not associate immediately with literary fun but who created her great detective by pondering the yet greater Sherlock Holmes is Agatha Christie. But in her 1929 book *Partners in Crime* she knocked off a couple of dozen parodies of the better-known sleuths of that day, ingeniously having her heroes, Tommy and Tuppence, take over a private enquiry office where on a shelf are a handful of detective stories. Tommy reads one and tackles the next crime that comes in, in the manner of the part.

Some of the targets have sunk into utter oblivion. Indeed, they had faded into such obscurity by the time Dame Agatha came to write her autobiography round about 1965 – the book was not published till 1977 – she said 'some of them by now I cannot even recognise. I remember Thornley Colton, the blind detective – Austin Freeman, of course'. Wrong, Dame A. Thornley Colton was the creation of one Clinton H. Stagg. But famous Holmes gets the treatment, of course, together with Austin Freeman's Dr Thorndyke – that's who, Dame Agatha – G.K. Chesterton's Father Brown, Baroness Orczy's Old Man in the Corner, A.E.W. Mason's Hanaud, Freeman Wills Crofts's Inspector French, Anthony Berkeley's Roger Sheringham, H.C. Bailey's Dr Reggie Fortune (his head scarcely above water now, rather undeservedly) and lastly her own Hercule Poirot. Altogether a mark of considerable versatility with words.

One of the cleverest and nicest parodies is Leo Bruce's *Case for Three Detectives*, originally written in 1936, hard to find in Britain nowadays but re-issued along with other Bruce books in paperback by Academy Chicago in America. Leo Bruce is the pseudonym used for his crime stories by Rupert Croft-Cooke, a novelist, playwright, poet and perhaps above all autobiographer. (His account of his days, evocative and interesting, runs into nearly 20 volumes.)

In *Case for Three* he produces a classic locked-room mystery and on the morning after the murder he has appear three of those 'indefatigably brilliant private investigators who seem to be always handy when a murder has been committed'. There is Monsignor Smith, who in character is not a mile away from Father Brown. There is Lord Simon Plimsoll, 'the length of whose chin like most other things about him was excessive' and who brings to mind, oddly enough, Lord Peter Wimsey. And there is Amer Picon – nice variant for Hercule Poirot – he of the 'large egg-shaped head, a head so much and so often egg-shaped that,' says the narrator, 'I was surprised to find a nose and mouth in it at all, but half-expected its white surface to break and release a chick.' Needless to say, none of the greats gets it right and the answer, which is actually satisfying, is provided by Bruce's regular Sergeant Beef, shrewd despite his look of beery benevolence.

Lord Peter, a tempting target if ever there was, has also been sharply dealt with in a collection by various hands called *Parody Party*, published in 1936, by none other than E.C. Bentley, of *Trent's Last Case*. He called his *jeu d'esprit* 'Greedy Night' and prefaced it with one of his clerihew verses (the 'C' of E.C. stands for 'Clerihew'):

> Lord Peter Wimsey
> May look a little flimsy,
> But he's simply sublime
> When nosing out a crime.

The story was neatly illustrated by the author's son, Nicholas Bentley, himself author of detective stories.

Very similar to *Case for Three Detectives* is another recently re-issued book, put out in Britain by the Pandora Press, a women's publishing house. But this is a case for *nine* detectives, *Murder in Pastiche* by Marion Mainwaring, originally written in 1955. Her nine, confined to a leaky tub of a ship, the *R.M.S. Florabunda*, first sighted chugging down a canal, are Trajan Beare, accompanied by leg-man Ernie Woodbin, Spike Bludgeon, Mallory King, Sir Joh: Nappleby, Jerry Pason, Atlas Poireau, Lord Simon Quinsey, Miss Fan Sliver and Broderick Tourneur. A moment's puzzling should tell you who the originals are. Read a few lines of Marion Mainwaring's farcical pages and you will catch instantly the portraits of the famous sleuths she hits off with fine neatness.

But the king of pasticheurs and president of parodists is surely Jon L. Breen, whose work has appeared mostly in *Ellery Queen's Mystery Magazine* over the years since 1967. The best of the many can be found – look long enough – in hard cover in *Hair of the Sleuthhound*, published on both sides of the Atlantic by the Scarecrow Press in 1982.

At the end of some of the pieces therein Mr Breen adds comments which his targets made to him. Typical of them is that from Ed McBain acknowledging a whole series of hits in the parody of his early *87th Precinct* books. 'One of the most difficult things in writing a continuing series,' he says, 'is to keep from parodying oneself . . . a piece like yours helps me once again to keep my eye on the sparrow.'

Presence of Body

What is better, asked *Punch* in the year 1849, than presence of mind in a railway accident? Answer: absence of body. But it is presence of body in, or thrown out of, a railway train that provides one of the better sub-genres of crime fiction. I think what lies at the heart of the extra fascination that crime on the line has is the contrast between the iron predictability of a rail journey and the inherent unpredictability of murder, between the implied control we have over our affairs symbolised in the timetable in contrast to the sudden unexpected ending of life that is murder.

There is, too, the isolation but not-isolation of the train. In the heyday of detective fiction in Britain trains had shut-away compartments holding at the most a dozen people. They were in isolation, and the train that was whirling them through (preferably) the night was in a second isolation. Yet, within that compartment, there was a little society, with its possible loves and hates and reasons for murder, and outside the train as it rattled along there, visible, was the whole society of the nation. The contrast, again, gave a certain extra dimension to any story of death on the railway.

So it is not surprising that the classic instances come from the great days of rail travel and chiefly from Britain where those closed compartments flourished. Indeed, the only American train crimes I can call to mind (though this probably only shows my comparative ignorance of American mystery fiction) are John Godey's *The Taking of Pelham 123*, which as the hijack of a subway train is not squarely in the rail crime situation, tense though its story was, and Patricia Highsmith's *Strangers on A Train*, which does no more than set its initial situation during a rail trip, though that does reflect on the isolation-cum-proximity that is one of the heightening factors of rail crime. Or there is Bill Pronzini's anthology *Midnight Specials*, published in America in 1977 and in Britain in 1978.

I even wonder whether the less atmospheric title of *Murder in the Calais Coach* for *Murder on the Orient Express* somehow reflects the fewer possibilities of American railroads, which, even in pre-plane days, were not unlike air travel. However, *Murder on the Orient Express* is surely the very best expression of the sub-genre. There you

Patricia Highsmith.

have the absolute isolation of the train caught in the snowdrift, with the inner isolation of the passengers in the murder coach blocked off reliably at each end from the rest of the train and with Hercule Poirot providentially among them. Plus the glamour of costly international travel and a millionaire (in the days when millionaires were not, so to speak, two a penny) and a princess and a count and a countess among the passenger suspects.

Agatha Christie herself was well aware of this glamour. In her autobiography she confesses that 'when I had travelled to France or Spain or Italy the Orient Express had often been standing at Calais, and I longed to climb up into it'. In fact, she nearly fell to her death in front of it on one occasion, as her second husband Sir Max Mallowan, the archaeologist, who actually suggested the startling solution of that locked-train mystery, recounts in his memoirs, adding laconically that a porter 'fished her up before the train started moving'.

The same romantic journey taken by Hercule Poirot, but in the opposite direction, comes in a very different book published in 1932 two years before the Christie opus, Graham Greene's *Stamboul Train*, called in America *Orient Express*. It is perhaps less a crime story than an espionage thriller, replete with the hinted violence, the fear behind the door, that marked Greene's early work so distinctively. He has said of the book that 'for the first and last time in my life I deliberately set out . . . to please', so I suppose crime fans can count it as one of theirs. But it was written under difficulties. The young Greene could not find the money to go by train all the way to Istanbul, though he had spent one day there some years earlier during a cruise. So to give himself the 'train feel' he repeatedly played a record of Honegger's piece 'Pacific 231'. The trick seems to have worked: the atmosphere of violence on the far side of the train's thin, frosted-over windows rises like mist from the pages.

Mrs Christie, of course, had not been content with that single venture into the delicious area of rail crime. We had in her earlier, sadder days immediately after her divorce from Colonel Christie *The Mystery of the Blue Train*, the famous Train Bleu of the 1920s taking the rich to the Riviera, along with 'a little man with an egg-shaped head', though she later said that the book was the worst she ever wrote.

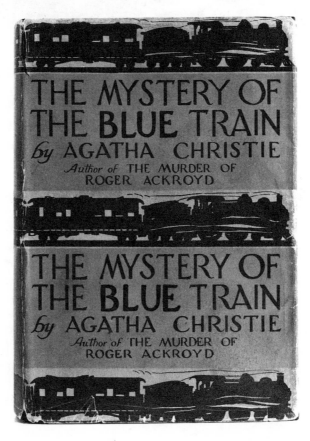

Still from *The Lady Vanishes* starring Margaret Lockwood and Michael Redgrave.

We had, too, in happier days *4.50 From Paddington* which certainly begins with the authentic rail crime situation when Mrs McGillicuddy (the US title was *What Mrs McGillicuddy Saw*) caught a glimpse of murder being committed in a train on a line parallel to hers. Splendid beginning, especially when she is not believed.

Indeed, there is only one more intriguing situation in railway crime – in what is perhaps the single rival to *Murder on the Orient Express*, Ethel Lina White's *The Wheel Spins*, known post-Hitchcock's film as *The Lady Vanishes*. Elderly, spinsterish Miss Froy disappears in a train that has not once stopped between the time the heroine exchanges a word or two with her and the time she is apparently no longer aboard. In part, no doubt, it is that marvellous situation that has kept the book alive over more than 50 years. In part, too, it owes its longevity to the movie. But in large part it is Ethel Lina White's excellent writing about real people that has been the salt that has preserved.

A fine railway crime story that has hardly survived, though it is well enough written and has a situation not far short of Ethel Lina White's in fascination, is *The Passenger from Scotland Yard*, written by a journalist, H.E. Wood, in 1888, and reprinted in 1977 in the excellent Dover Publications series with an introduction by the learned and lively E.F. Bleiler. It begins very promisingly. 'The night mail for the Continent stood ready to glide out of the London terminus . . .', and then puts a late-arriving fifth passenger into one of its compartments which, as was then customary, the guard locks up. When the train reaches Paris it is revealed that one of the five in the compartment is a Yard detective, another is an undetected murderer and a third is a corpse. Now read on . . .

What can be done in the large, can also be done in the little. To prove which, we have in a very short story by Edmund Crispin 'Beware of the Trains', a marvellously puzzling 'locked-station' story. Crispin envisaged a country station surrounded by chance and with good reason by police, and into it there arrives a train whose driver then simply disappears. Within ten pages Crispin manages to lay out this situation, to give us an absolutely convincing final explanation and to put in a strong dash of real railway atmosphere. 'A whistle blew; jolting slightly, the big posters on the hoardings took themselves off rearwards – and with sudden acceleration, like a thrust in the back, the electric train moved out of Borleston Junction . . .' It may not be the romance of steam, but at once we are deep in the genuine, enclosed, forward-moving train world.

Though for a train atmosphere evoked at greater length, teetering indeed on the edge of too great length, there is nowhere better to go than to the opening chapter of Michael Innes's most farcical novel *Appleby's End*. No murder is committed on the train in question, nor as it turns out is one committed at all, much though it is threatened when Inspector Appleby arrives at the halt named Appleby's End. But the feel of a railway journey through cold and dark English countryside is impressed deep into my memory. Perhaps, indeed, it was responsible for a very different rail journey, through sun-scintillating India, I wrote of myself in *Inspector Ghote Goes By Train*.

So much for atmosphere and the isolation factor. But when we come to the regularity-*v*-chaos aspect there is one name that leaps head and shoulders to the fore, Freeman Wills Crofts. Crofts began his days, in fact, if not as a railway administrator at least as chief assistant engineer eventually to the Belfast and Northern Counties Railway. And when after an illness he took to crime writing, he brought to his work all the precision of the engineer, all the solid virtues of the best sort of Ulster Protestant.

So in due course we got Inspector French, unrelenting in his checking of alibi against timetable until his criminal was brought to

justice. Let's have a taste of him unpicking an alibi by reconstructing a murder on a train. It's from *Sir John Magill's Last Journey*. 'I now,' French says to his stand-in victim, 'crack your brainbox.' Then he dresses him in a brown cloak, waits for the train to make a regular but unscheduled short stop, flings a rope-ladder out and pushes the 'victim' out after. Now he waits for the substitute who will 'prove' the victim alive at a later time. 'What if the thing had miscarried? And then French heard the whistle of the guard, and the train slowly began to move. Curse! Something had gone wrong! No, it hadn't though! The ladder shook again and the ropes strained tight.' Lovely stuff.

Brown Studies

Detective literature, Dr Erik Routley, author of *The Puritan Pleasures of the Detective Story*, remarks 'is seventy-five per cent moralism anyhow.' So, he argues, it is no bad thing to have a minister of religion as a fictional detective. He was writing, of course, about G.K. Chesterton's Father Brown, who came eventually to lead a whole troop of pastors of various religions taking time from their spiritual duties to settle a few earthly murders.

By and large these religious sleuths align themselves with the secular detectives of their day. Thus Father Brown, who to an extent must have been created in reaction to Sherlock Holmes, the coldly scientific, is clearly nevertheless like Holmes a Great Detective. You have only to look at his own description of his method to see it.

In one of the later tales 'The Secret of Father Brown' an American visitor to Spain, where the little Norfolk priest is staying – Father

WHAT ISN'T IN A NAME

If Anthony Boucher, critic and crime novelist (real name: William Anthony Parker White) adopted the pseudonym of a notorious mass-murderer, H.H. Holmes (real name: Hermann Webster Mudgett) for some of his stories, other crime writers have not lagged far behind in choosing other odd names under which to write. I suppose the most extraordinary is that adopted by the father of Japanese mystery fiction who called himself Edogawa Rampo (i.e. Edgar Allen Poe). But others follow close behind.

There's the lady who publishes in America as E.X. Ferrars. The X stands for an unknown factor and was provided only in answer to a stern request for her second name. In Britain she's just Elizabeth Ferrars, and in real life (which is different from Britain or America) she is Morna Brown. To her, one can add A.A. Fair (Erle Syanley Gardner) both of whose initials stand for nothing, as do the S.S. of S.S. Van Dine (Willard Huntington Wright), creator of Philo Vance.

X seems to be a fair favourite when authors look for a second name under which to produce those few extra (X-tra) books. For example, there's Bill Pronzini, very prolific of short stories and a pretty good producer of novels. A good many of his come from 'Jack Foxx'. Yes, with two xs. And he's also Alex Saxon. And actually as well Brett Halliday, William Jeffrey and John Barry Williams. There is, too, Professor Francis Smith who styles himself as a mystery novelist S.F.X. Dean.

And high up on my odd pseudonym prize list comes Robert L. Fish. He, disguised with fiendish cunning, is also Robert L. Pike, and A.C. Lamprey. And best for most useful pen-name? Well, when Ms Carolyn Heilbrun was seeking academic tenure, so the story goes, she didn't want the Stuffies to know she had written 'a mere detective story'. So it was Amanda Cross (and that's surely an X too) who gave us *In the Last Analysis* and its delightful follow-ups while Professor Heilbrun lived to flourish in academe.

Brown moves around the world at the whim of his Creator, or perhaps his creator – challenges him thus:

> We are well acquainted with the alleged achievements of Dupin and others; and with those of Lecoq, Sherlock Holmes, Nicholas Carter and other imaginative incarnations of the craft. But we observe there is in many ways a marked difference between your own method of approach and that of these other thinkers.

Father Brown of course modestly disclaims having any method but eventually brings himself to say, 'I try to get inside the murderer . . . thinking his thoughts, wrestling with his passions; till I have bent myself into the posture of his hunched and peering hatred . . . Till I am really a murderer.' Then, he says, he knows. And then, too, he has shown himself to be precisely at one with Dupin, whom Edgar Allan Poe compared to the most successful player of board games, someone capable of throwing 'himself into the spirit of his opponent, identifying himself therewith'.

Plainly, too, Father Brown's contemporary, first appearing in America only some seven years later, Melville Davisson Post's Uncle Abner, is another Great Detective, who if he is not an ordained minister is a man steeped in the Bible. Like Sherlock Holmes, he solves his mysteries after entering into a kind of trance, taking on 'a deep, strange look'. This is Holmes's pipe smoke-wreathed contemplation in which he united the discoveries of the left brain and the right brain to produce what Poe called that 'which has never occurred before'. Abner, great quoter of the Bible, is different indeed from Father Brown, great producer of paradoxes. But they are one in bringing detective fiction that 75 per cent of moralism that gives its best products backbone.

This cannot really be said of Canon Victor L. Whitechurch's the Rev Harry Westerham, investigating vicar of *The Crime at Diana's Pool*. But we have now reached 1926 and detection-as-fun is the spirit of the times. In four years time the newly founded Collins Crime Club in London is to appoint the Rev Dr Cyril Argentine Alington, who will go on to become Dean of Durham, as one of its expert panel choosing the club's titles. The Rev Harry Westerman is eminently sensible and a dab hand at a church fête. But those are qualities the Great Detective managed without.

Altogether sharper was the nun-detective Sister Ursula, of the (fictional) Order of Martha of Bethany, the creation of Anthony Boucher under his H.H. Holmes pseudonym. She is to be found (but

not, alas, in Britain) in five short stories he wrote and two novels, 'locked-room' mysteries, *Nine Times Nine* in 1940, a book that incorporates a discussion of 'impossible crime' mysteries taking off from John Dickson Carr's famed Chapter 17 in *The Three Coffins* (also known as *The Hollow Man*) and *Rocket to the Morgue* in 1942, wherein a number of the author's friends from the world of sci-fi are depicted *à*, as the French say, *clef*.

Neither does Thurman Warriner's Archdeacon Toft with his assistant sleuth that very proper gentleman, Mr Ambo (an ambo, in case you don't know, is a raised platform in an early Christian church, and its plural is 'ambones') qualify as any sort of Great Detective, not even tripled up with the brash private investigator, Scotter. But the books that feature them, written in the 1950s, with their strong theme of good battling with evil and their distrust of religious fundamentalism, have certainly got 75 per cent of moralism in their make-up.

We cross the Atlantic again next to ponder Father Bredder, who began his sleuthing career in Leonard Holton's *The Saint Maker* in 1959. Though Holton, whose real name was Leonard Wibberley and who wrote a charming fantasy *The Mouse That Roared* as such, was a native of Dublin and educated partly in England, only three of the Father Bredder stories were published in Britain. Aiming to write more in the manner of Dorothy L. Sayers than in the Hammett or in the Ian Fleming style ('I'm not fond of bashing people around'), he wanted to devise 'a nonfussy and nonviolent' sleuth and thought that a priest would fit the bill. But he did make his Franciscan a former marine and a skilled amateur boxer.

Religion features centrally in the first of his cases when Father Bredder at last catches up with a nice old lady who kills people when they are in a state of grace immediately after Confession so that they will go directly to Heaven. Father Bredder is very much a priest of his day, much concerned with charity in the form of visiting seamy flophouse hotels and less interested, perhaps, in faith in the way that Father Brown was. He smokes a cheap Carolina tobacco and cannot bring himself to invest in a pouch for it, preferring a paper envelope. He does, however, buy an occasional old novel for a quarter, but only when he feels he is flush with money.

Next in chronological order of their book appearances, though by far the earliest in the time at which he sleuthed, comes Ellis Peters's Brother Cadfael, herbalist in the twelfth century monastery of Shrewsbury. He was, perhaps, created in response to the 1960s and 1970s restless search for ever-new variants on the detective. Certainly Ellis Peters had written a good many crime stories with various detectives earlier. There was Inspector Felse and different members of his family acting independently. On a couple of occasions there was even an Indian guru. But at last she hit on Brother Cadfael and eventually enormous success.

She owed some of that success – but she has merits galore, fine atmosphere, clever plots, impeccable historical detail – to an extraordinary publishing phenomenon which has been claimed for mystery fiction, Umberto Eco's long and learned novel *The Name of the Rose*, which came out in English from its original Italian in 1983 and swept the bookstalls everywhere. Certainly the book has a 'detective' hero, an English friar, William of Baskerville (Shades of . . .), and he does investigate murder, in an Italian abbey of the fourteenth century. But the novel aims at being a lot more than a detective story, and it is not really right to claim it for crime.

In the same year that Ellis Peters's first Brother Cadfael story, *A Morbid Taste for Bones*, came out, 1977, there appeared in America the first case of an altogether contemporary priest-detective Ralph McInerny's *Her Death of Cold*, featuring Father Roger Dowling. Father Dowling, stooped, thinning-haired, pipe-smoking and by no means fully in favour of the changes in his Church in recent years, is a former alcoholic who for a long stretch had been a

Canon lawyer examining cases for annulment of marriage (good for logic). His creator has said of him that he may seem soft on crime but that he is hard on sin. It is not every sleuth who say of the murderer he is tracking down that they must come to recognise the sinfulness of what they have done, 'ask God's pardon for the deed, repent'.

But, not content with having given us one religious detective, Roger McInerny took the pen-name of Monica Quill and produced another. This time it was a nun, Mother Mary Teresa, a crime-solver her creator cheerfully labels as 'an aged female curmudgeon, what Nero Wolfe might have been if he had taken the veil'. Now, that's a lovely thought.

Decidedly contemporary, however, is Rabbi David Small, the unassuming, bespectacled, stooping and soft-spoken, though steel-backboned, part-time crime solver invented by Harry Kemelman in 1964 with *Friday the Rabbi Slept Late*, a book that leapt to fame with a Mystery Writers of America Edgar Allan Poe Award. The series lasted until 1979 when with *Thursday the Rabbi Walked Out* Kemelman ran out of days of the week. The stories are remarkable for what they tell us of the workings of a small-town Jewish community in Massachusetts. They have been called 'a sparkling and provocative compound of fact and fabrication'.

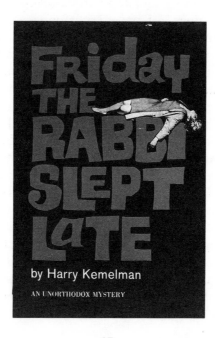

A similar feat was attempted by a former Roman Catholic priest, William Kienzle, who created much in his own image Father Robert Koesler, in *The Rosary Murders* in 1974. The series had grown to five books ten years later. Father Koesler is, as was his creator, a diocesan priest in Detroit and editor of a weekly Roman Catholic paper. He is, Mr Kienzle has said, the same age, height and build as himself and has a similar philosophy of life. In stories he sees as being in the traditional British-style who-done-it mould, Mr Kienzle depicts life in a Roman Catholic parish in Detroit. Suffice it to say, it is a far cry from the days and duties of Father Brown.

Hissing Mysteries

There have been mystery stories set in historical times from the very earliest days of the art, and even from before then if you count Charles Dickens's story 'A Confession Found in A Prison in the Time of Charles II', seized on and improved by Edgar Allan Poe in 'The Tell-tale Heart'. Both of these, however, are really murder stories (that is stories simply about a murder) rather than crime stories or mysteries (in which there is something to be solved). But if we are thinking of proper historical mystery stories then way ahead of all other periods of time in popularity are the books set in Victorian days, the days of the melodrama villains born to be hissed.

So put aside Agatha Christie's *Death Comes at the End* (Ancient Egypt), Ellis Peters's chronicles of Brother Cadfael (twelfth century), Josephine Tey's *The Daughter of Time* (the Princes in the Tower, at one remove), Aristotle and Socrates as detectives (Margaret Doody's novel and a couple of short stories by Breni James in the 1950s) and the Great Lexicographer as Great Detective in Lillian de la Torre's *Dr Sam: Johnson Detector*. Put that aside even though it was hailed by Ellery Queen as 'the finest of historical detective stories ever written – in scholarship, humour, flavour and compelling detail' and let us wallow briefly in Victorian villainies.

JACK THE GRIPPER

Besides *The Lodger*, Mrs Belloc Lowndes' novel springing from the Jack the Ripper murders in London's East End in 1888 and 1889, whose killings caused an immense sensation at the time and have never since ceased to hold the public even though by the standards of mass-murder the six crimes are small beer, dozens of fictional works have taken the Ripper as their hero—villain. Sometimes his tale has been re-told with a few extra imported elements; sometimes Jack has been lifted to another age, even another universe.

As early as 1892, in Finland of all places, the first Ripper rip-off appeared, a collection of short stories. It was promptly suppressed by the Russian censor. In 1895 the well-known German playwright Wedekind produced his *Der Erdgeist* featuring the Ripper and he followed it in 1904 with *Die Buchse der Pandora*, from both of which Allan Berg fashioned his opera *Lulu*, in which Jack is Lulu's last pick-up as a prostitute and her murderer.

Leaping the years, we come to Thomas Burke's short story 'The Hands of Mr Ottermole', hailed in 1949 by a jury which included John Dickson Carr and Ellery Queen as 'the greatest mystery story of all time'. Jack Triumphant. And in 1966 Ellery Queen himself joined the fiction Ripperologists with *Sherlock Holmes Versus Jack the Ripper* (in America more prosaically *A Study in Terror*), though perhaps the book as a novelisation of a film should hardly be counted in the Queen canon.

Equally, Robert Bloch, author of *Psycho*, that classic, may be a little ashamed of his 1984 book *Night of the Ripper* ('Stop me before I write more,' he once pleaded) which piles in so much local colour and so many possible suspects that laughter is perhaps the only possible reaction. Yet he wrote an excellent short story on the theme, 'Yours Truly, Jack the Ripper.'

Maybe, though, the final word should go to Michael Dibdin's *The Last Sherlock Holmes Story* (it won't be: Holmes and the Ripper are too tempting). In it the Great Detective is revealed as being Guess Who.

Peter Lovesey, who wrote some of the best Victorian mysteries in his books about Sergeant Cribb and his more recent *Bertie and the Tinman* (His Royal Highness Edward, Prince of Wales, and Fred Archer, jockey), has suggested that the period is so popular with crime writers and crime readers partly because of its real crimes like 'Jack the Ripper stalking the foggy streets of Whitechapel' and partly because the ethos of the period provided splendid motives for murder, the stigmas of divorce, insanity and scandal with the favoured method of poison, slow and insidious. I might add that the Victorian era is the nearest time to our day looking backward when people were recognisably like ourselves – the men wore trousers, wigs were out – and yet interestingly different. One might say, too, that nastiness put into the past is apt to become nostalgic niceness.

In them thar days, of course, your police investigator in England was no Detective Chief Superintendent but often a humble sergeant, like Cribb. Or like Sergeant Verity, portly and plodding, in the series of books by Francis Selwyn in which the Verity name always appears in the title. On one occasion Sergeant Verity even gets to meet the famous Sergeant Cuff, of Wilkie Collins's *The Moonstone*.

Wilkie Collins himself is the detective in one of John Dickson Carr's historical crime stories that falls within the Victorian period. Beside *The Hungry Goblin*, Carr's nineteenth-century novels include that fine story *The Bride of Newgate*, set in 1815, and *Fire, Burn!* about the establishment of the first detective, as opposed to preventive, police in London in 1829. Then there is *The Scandal at High Chimneys*, an 1865 story featuring the real Inspector Whicher, who failed over the real Constance Kent case, only to be vindicated later.

There is, too, in Carr's output, if we leak a little into Edwardian England, *The Witch at Low Tide*, an 'impossible crime' situation in the bathing-tent (there's ingenuity). And, whisking back to Carr's native America, we have *Papa La Bas*, set in New Orleans in 1858 and whiffing of voodoo.

While we are in America we have the murder of a prostitute in Raymond Paul's 1982 book, *The Thomas Street Horror*, followed in 1984 by *Tragedy at Tiverton*, telling of the first American minister of religion to be tried for murder. In Britain that story is paralleled by Julian Symons's *Sweet Adelaide*, a fictional reconstruction of the Pimlico murder case in which Adelaide Bartlett stood trial for the murder of her husband by administering chloroform by mouth, and the Rev George Dyson, who bought the chloroform, was lucky not to be standing beside her in the dock. Julian Symons has also written two fine historical crime novels set just beyond the Victorian period, *The Blackheath Poisonings* and *The Detling Murders*.

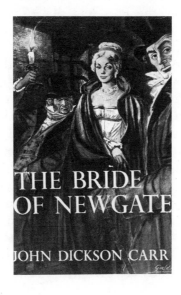

To these we might tag on, since we have crept out of Queen Victoria's days, the work of a new writer, Michael Pearce. He has begun what is expected to be a long series about the Mamur Zapt (it deserves success for that name alone), the head of Cairo's secret police in 1908, one Captain Cadwallader Owen. The signs are hopeful.

But how about a murder mystery centring on that quiet poet, Emily Dickinson (in whose house at Amherst, Massachusetts, Julian Symons once resided, circularity indeed)? When Jane Langton's book first came out in 1964 it was called *The Transcendental Murder*. Now it is *The Minutemen Murder* and it has been followed in 1984 by *Emily Dickinson Is Dead*. Is no one sacred from the mystery writer's pen? Well, no, not judging by a splendid romp by Robert Player, *Oh! Where Are Bloody Mary's Earrings?* set among the British royal family in the days when Bertie (of Peter Lovesey's book) was strapped for cash and coveted that regal heirloom.

Nor are Presidents, or at least future Presidents, safe. Lawrence Alexander's *The Big Stick* starred Teddy Roosevelt (as did William De Andrea's *The Lunatic Fringe* and H. Paul Jeffers's *The Adventure of the Stalwart Companion*). In 1885 the future President headed the New York Police Department Board and the opportunity to show him as sleuth was evidently too good to miss, especially when his cousin, Franklin D. could be seen getting threatening letters signed with a black hand. But George Washington, even, has been made to play detective in a story in *Ellery Queen's Mystery Magazine* by Stephen Peters while the President of Texas before it joined the Union, Sam Houston, was also 'detectivised' in the same magazine by James C. Brough.

An American equally distinguished received the same treatment in Theodore Mathieson's novel *The Devil and Ben Franklin*. Mathieson is a great history mystery man. In short stories he en-sleuthed Captain Cook, Defoe, Cortez, Alexander the Great, Cervantes, Omar Khayyam, Stanley and Livingstone together, Florence Nightingale, Daniel Boone and Galileo.

And, fun still to the fore, look at Elizabeth Peters's 1981 book *The Curse of the Pharoahs*, in which her redoubtable Amelia Peabody Emerson wields her parasol 'of stout bombazine with a steel shaft' to fine effect and at the last minute unmasks the hatpin murderesss, Lady Baskerville. (What other name could she have had?) In an earlier adventure, *Crocodile on the Sandbank*, Ms Peters illuminates for us nineteenth-century Egyptology.

Still with something of the frolic about it, though with a gruesome enough murder, is R.J. White's *The Smartest Grave*, co-winner of the competition for a detective story written by a don in 1961. This deals with a real murder case, in Essex in 1899 when a forger and con-man Samuel Dougal made away with his much older wife. F. Tennyson Jesse edited the volume in the *Notable British Trials* series which deals with the case. It included evidence that during the four years while Dougal's victim remained buried on his farm he brought a number of girls there to teach them to ride the newly invented bicycle. This, he persuaded them, was best done without the benefit of clothes. 'What a picture,' Miss Tennyson Jesse wrote, 'in that clayey, lumpy field, the clayey, lumpy girls, naked, astride that unromantic object, a bicycle.'

Into the category of romp-plus-something-more I put a delightful *jeu d'esprit* by Gwendoline Butler. In the 1970s she was writing odd and interesting books with as hero a Scotland Yard man named Coffin, generally with his evocative name in her title. But her 1973 book *A Coffin for Pandora* (*Olivia*, of course in America) is set, not in contemporary Britain, but in nineteenth-century Oxford, with Mrs Humphrey Ward, bestseller of her day, flashing intriguingly across a page if I remember rightly. The book won the Silver Dagger of the Crime Writers Association in Britain, but it did not feature Inspector Coffin, or even his grandfather.

Inspectors – in Britain they are a good deal lowlier than in the American police forces – did begin to feature eventually in historical crime stories set in Victorian days in England. We have Inspector Lintott in Jean Stubbs's 1973 book *Dear Laura* set in the 1890s, described so meticulously you might well believe this fiction is non-fiction. He also appears in some follow-up volumes. Then there is Anne Perry's Inspector Thomas Pitt, who in *The Cater Street Hangman*, his first outing, is treated with all the lack of respect proper to the police of Victorian days (but does get to marry a witness, equally properly a victim of Victorian repressiveness). The book is set in the days of the Jack the Ripper murders, though it is primarily concerned with the effect on people near the scene. An equally offbeat treatment of the Ripper is to be found in a much earlier book, Mrs Belloc Lowndes's *The Lodger* written in 1913 and several times filmed.

That's our patch – long may it find crime writers to embroider it.

Dead Funny

Murder shouldn't be comical, and I suppose if you happened to get murdered you'd hardly find it a hoot. But it cannot be denied that corpses and comedy somehow go very nicely together. I think, to look on the lofty side for a moment, that it is perhaps a good thing: being a little shocked by a joke about something appalling makes it easier to cope with a similar appallingness if at some future time you should find yourself involved.

So, from at least Sherlock Holmes onwards, the comic has had its part to play in crime fiction. Dr Watson unerringly pinpoints Professor Presley's four-legged monkey-gait in 'The Creeping Man' as the effect of lumbago and 'Good, Watson,' Holmes cries, 'You always keep us flat-footed to the ground.' But that is simply a relieving flash of humour, only a little less large in scope than Shakespeare's use of the Porter's dreadful drunken jokes in *Macbeth* as a prelude to the murder. Or, at the other side of a tense situation, there are Nigel Strangeways' nonsense questions when he arrives on the scene of the true-to-life death in Nicholas Blake's *The Beast Must*

Die. Cecil Day Lewis – Blake's real name – has told how the idea for the book sprang from his own son narrowly escaping a hit-and-run driver.

But the comic can play a much larger part in mystery fiction. Indeed, that looming literary pundit, Northrop Frye, in his *Anatomy of Criticism*, pointed out that at least all the cosy detective stories, all those in which the murderer is brought to justice, ought to be called (with stern capitals) Comic Fictional Modes. He's right too.

So let's take a quick sweep through the field. Starting from the top, if you like, with wit, with those crime stories whose actual main interest lies not in who done it but more in how many sharp points can be made between page 1 and page 220. A few quick examples: Julian Symons's *The Man Who Lost His Wife*, a book that rises to a hilarious scathingness; almost all the Raymond Chandler books (Moose Malloy 'was a big man, but not more than six feet five inches tall and not wider than a beer truck'); almost all the books, come to that, of Michael Innes (the character in *Sheiks and Adders* who comes to the fancy-dress party, 'a spectacle of the most horrendous and revolting sort', as one of the Seven Deadly Sins, which one undecided); or – the list could be much, much longer – Amanda Cross's Professor Kate Fansler in *The Theban Mysteries* with 'Shifting problems is the first rule for a long and pleasant life.'

Then there is the humour, typically English, of gentle deflation. So, let that most typical of English writers, Dame Agatha Christie, provide our key example. I could choose from a fair number of gentle gibes, but try this: Ariadne Oliver, famous crime novelist, talking about her protagonist, Sven Hjerson, 'If I ever met that bony, gangling, vegetable-eating Finn in real life, I'd do a much better murder than any I've ever invented.' A left-and-a-right from the, as it were, tweed-clad, shotgun-wielding author for, first, Agatha Christie herself, and, second, plump, short, gourmet Hercule Poirot.

A whole sub-branch of this sort of gentle humour is to be found in the British use of long words where short ones would do. (Americans, let me snarl, use very long words where long ones would serve, to achieve not comicality but solemnity.)

Perhaps the trick is a little played out nowadays, but in the Golden Age . . . There is Edmund Crispin having one of his dons say, instead of 'take a leak' or whatever, 'in pursuance, I imagine, of some bodily necessity'. Or there is Gladys Mitchell's chapter title 'A Multiplicity of Promiscuous Vessels'. I think they were chamber-pots, always good for a giggle in those dear, distant days. Indeed, E.C. Bentley, in that early, odd classic of detective stories, *Trent's Last Case*, specifically comments through Trent on the long words idea. 'A people like our own,' he says of Britons,

> not very fond of using its mind, get on in the ordinary way with a very small and simple vocabulary. Long words are abnormal, and like everything else that is abnormal, they are either very funny or tremendously solemn ... There's 'terminological inexactitude'. How we all roared, and are still roaring at that. And the whole of the joke is that the words are long.

On to that it would not be unfair to tack the trick of using comical names, only noting that they do have another function beyond that of raising a passing smile. They establish a general lightness of touch. As you come across the comical names piled one on the other, you know this is going to be a book where tracking down a murderer is not a very serious business.

Thus Michael Innes gives us such places as the Forest of Drool, Sneak, Snarl, Yatter and Boxer's Bottom together with people saddled with such surnames as Beaglehole, Scurl, Grope, Twist and Fancroft, Wedge, Gotlop, Alspach and Ffolliott Petticate. And, be it noted, rather later an American writer like Charlotte MacLeod has at her regular Balaclava Agricultural College setting Heidi Heyhoe, the student siren, Idura Bjorklund, Amazonian heiress from South Dakota, college president Hjalmar Olaffsen and Fred Ottermole, chief of police, not to speak of Cronkite Swope, ace reporter from the county weekly, and her charming sleuth himself, Professor Shandy.

Books like hers are only a little way off the whole class of crime stories that could fly under the banner 'Murder Is Fun'. I don't know whether nowadays we have actually come to regard people killing people as something on the whole not very funny, but it is a fact that the majority of books under the pure 'Fun' banner were written before World War II, though contemporary examples are to be found. Indeed, the phenomenon was more or less strictly a between-wars occurrence with the first notable example being the jokey whodunnit *The Red House Mystery* by A.A. Milne. (Should he have stuck to Pooh Bear?) In that book, when the utterly amateur detective announces he's going to solve the murder, his about-to-be Watson at once exclaims, 'What fun!'

But even the greats of that age were apt on occasion to emphasise the sheer fun of sudden mortality. There are, for instance, the Tommy and Tuppence books of Agatha Christie, starting with *The Secret Adversary*, another 1922 book, and perhaps going on right up

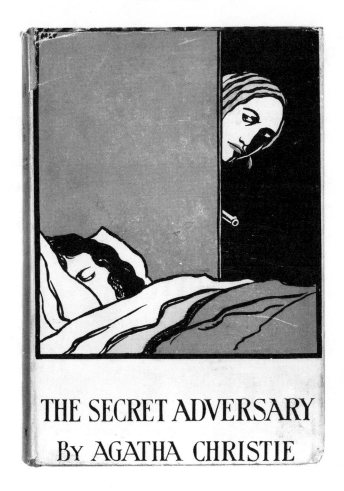

to their appearance, on the border of senility, in 1973 in *Postern of Fate*. When in *Partners in Crime*, their second outing, our happy pair are put in charge of a detective agency – by Britain's top spy-hunter, no less –Tuppence exclaims delightedly, 'It will be too marvellous . . . We will hunt down murderers.'

Not to be outdone, Dorothy L. Sayers in *Whose Body?* famously has Lord Peter's manservant Bunter say when another corpse is found, 'Indeed, my lord. That's very gratifying.' That was in 1923. Later Lord Peter became more serious about catchin' the odd murderer, what – and the books, I think, became less good.

To go down a step from the fun brigade we can perhaps see ourselves as entering the realm of knock-about, essentially the humour of the stage double act. This, of course, can vary from the reasonably subtle to the rollickingly crude. At the subtle end we

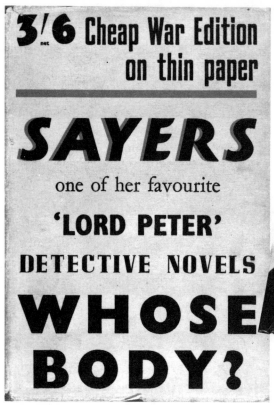

have the most famous comic team of all mystery fiction, rivalled indeed in all fiction only by Don Quixote and Sancho Panza, Holmes and Watson. Among the many useful attributes of Conan Doyle's discovery of the Watson was the opportunities that relationship presented for lightening touches of humour. Even that most quoted of all exchanges between the two of them, the one that has the crushing punch-line of 'That was the curious incident', after Watson's innocent 'The dog did nothing in the night-time', has more of a comic put-down about it than of an investigative advance.

It is very nearly what Craig Rice, a lady who was in her day among the most successful writers of humorous hard-boiled stories, once called 'that unbeatable vaudeville team of the shrewd detective and the comic cop'. Examples pop up in the mind, Poirot and Inspector Japp, Stuart Palmer's schoolmistress Hildegard Withers and poor Inspector Piper – here we are at the crude end of the spectrum – and Miss Marple and Inspector Neele of *A Pocket Full of Rye*, the policeman who was 'a highly imaginative thinker ... one of his methods of investigation was to propound himself fantastic theories of guilt which he applied to such persons as he was investigating'. (But then Mrs Christie's first husband had run off with a Miss Neele.)

From the knock-about let us descend to, or perhaps take off into, farce. Now we are in doubly tricky territory. Not only do our authors have to juggle with the delicate counterpoise of murder and mirth, they also have to struggle with the threat posed by the absurd to the essentially realist business of finding the killer and by the equal threat poised by the logic of the hunt to the bubbling airiness of pure farce.

To my mind no one does this better than Donald E. Westlake. He seems to have secured for himself all the talents necessary to bring off the tricky feat. First, he has realised, as the great French masters of theatre farce did, that to make your flights into the fantastic still somehow plausible you have to start from a base of plain ordinariness. Take, for instance, *Nobody's Perfect*, which is going to involve its bungling burglar Dortmunder in events taking place in a highly unlikely Scottish castle. It begins in a soberly likely New York courthouse interview cubicle 'with its institutional green walls, its black linoleum floor ... its battered wooden table and two battered chairs and one battered metal waste basket'. Zola himself couldn't have been more down-to-earth.

Then Westlake chooses his words always with scrupulous care, yet more necessary, paradoxically, in the rumbustious world he takes us into than in calmer places. His poised see-saw must not thump heavily down on to one side or the other, ugly crime or rootless laughter. And next he gives us action a-plenty, so that reading you never have time to stop and think, 'Hey, this is altogether impossible.' Instead, you just get a feeling that it is all delightfully ridiculous, a feeling that lasts long after the books is finished.

Equally, a writer very much less rough-and-tumble, and from the British side of the Atlantic naturally, Edmund Crispin, still uses action, chiefly in the form of chases, to keep the reader from thinking too much. This he does even in stories set amid the academic calm of Oxford, such as the wild careering through the city's streets, beginning at that part of the river called Parsons' Pleasure where naked male bathing was permitted, that forms the final pages of *The Moving Toyshop*. And in his swansong book, *The Glimpses of the Moon*, Crispin even contrived a farcical chase that runs to over 40 pages and incorporates the local hunt, a band of hunt

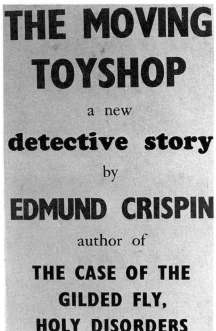

saboteurs, a herd of cows and a passing group of motor-cycle maniacs, not to speak of an electricity pylon that conveniently explodes, a strong-box that has been booby-trapped and as many assorted policemen as you will.

Then, of course, almost as effective as a good chase in whoomping up the atmosphere of utter farce, while still keeping a thread of detection going, is a good fight. How about the fracas involving the television crew and a pair of union stalwarts in Simon Brett's *Situation Tragedy*? The glazed chicken wings of the party spread fly through the air. The whizzing coleslaw ends thickly matting hair all round. But then there is a ringing scream. And a body is found for Brett's actor sleuth, Charles Paris, ineptly to investigate.

Ineptly, but successfully. Because farce crime, however farcical it is, has also to stay within the canons of whatever particular branch of crime fiction it has put itself. Charles Paris is in the tradition of the amateur detective, and as such it is his creator's duty to have him in the end find out who done it. Where comic crime fails is when, as does sometimes happen, the writer forgets this golden rule. Then it's no joke.

Breakfast, Lunch and Tea

Sex. I suppose, is the staple of the contemporary crime story. It was not ever thus. In the days when almost the nearest thing to sexual involvement that the crime story (or the detective story as it was then) reached was a 'Darling, it's all over, he said', there was something that played a very much more important part in the telling. Meals. They run like a doughy thread through the books of what has been called the Golden Age of the detective story.

Your really implacable sleuth in the English books of the 1930s could never go far without pausing to eat the appropriate meal. Take the works of Freeman Wills Crofts, great specialist in alibis and false alibis, and, to tell the truth, a producer of prose almost as stodgy as the meals it described. Here is his Inspector French in *Sir John Magill's Last Journey* (a book still pleasurable, if drily so) when a sergeant comes to announce an important discovery: 'Come and have a bite of breakfast and then let's have the great news.'

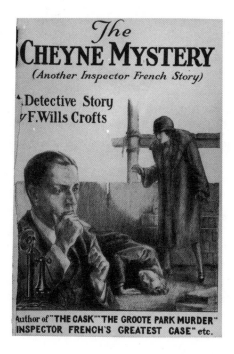

Breakfast, indeed, was perhaps the greatest slower-up of murder investigation (though it should not be forgotten that in a certain sort of book slowing-up is what the reader wants; it infuriates, but delightfully so). And the great breakfast delay can be seen as starting at the very beginning of crime fiction. In Wilkie Collins's marvellous *The Moonstone* you find dear old Gabriel Betteredge, house steward to Lady Verinder, saying 'We had our breakfast – whatever happens in a house, robbery or murder, it doesn't matter, you must have your breakfast.' Collins, in fact, was using necessary, everyday breakfast as just one flick in the grand symbolic contrast between the illusory and the real that ballasts his whole wonderfully readable story.

Other, later authors were less cunning. Breakfast for them was simply breakfast. Georgette Heyer took time off from her Regency romances to write a dozen detective stories one of which was called significantly *Why Shoot the Butler?* (butler, bringer of food to the table). In *Behold, Here's Poison* after the murder has been committed she writes of the housekeeper, Mrs Beecher, being given 'a great many orders . . . for the subsequent using-up of the fish and eggs already cooked for a breakfast . . . no one could think of eating.'

While in *Death of A Millionaire*, one of the 29 detective stories from the scarcely ever-resting pens (severe tomes as well as crime) of the man-and-wife team of G.D.H. and Margaret Cole, we get Lord Ealing declining breakfast at Sugden's Hotel when his fellow breaker of the fast is found missing from his blood-splattered bedroom. Happily the hotel manager does say, 'I have taken the liberty, my lord,' and indicates a tray on which reposes a plate of sandwiches together with whisky and soda. But it is an American, Leslie Ford, writing as David Frome, who gets it really right in *The Murder on the Sixth Hole* of 1931 by having sleuth Major Lewis delay inspecting the corpse on the course, saying 'I felt that breakfast was more important just then.'

Though perhaps an acceptable compromise is to be found in a book by George Birmingham (Canon J.O. Hannay) in the 1920s, *Wild Justice*. Here the Chief Constable is adamant that 'all statements should be taken in the library' sternly rejecting the amateur sleuths' plea, 'If you'd listen to what Bastable has to say in the dining-room we could eat while he is talking.' In the end, however, he does allow the butler, his tale told, to serve some breakfast in the library while members of the household higher in the social scale are privately questioned.

Perhaps the classic breakfast in crime fiction, however, comes in that book intended as a put-down of the genre which became a classic in its own right, E.C. Bentley's *Trent's Last Case*. Chapter III there is headed simply 'Breakfast' and in it we read of Mr Nathaniel Burton Cupples deciding that the previous day's excitements, the murder of the millionaire Sigsbee Manderson no less, merit 'a third piece of toast and an additional egg'. Soon he is joined by that very young-man-of-the-period Trent, exclaiming, 'Why sit'st thou by that ruined breakfast? Dost thou its former pride recall, or ponder how it passed away?' before he in his turn demands 'an enormous breakfast' and when it arrives shows 'an unaffected interest in the choice of food'.

Illustration from the first edition of *Trent's Last Case* perhaps responsible for the American title *The Woman in Black*.

That was in 1913. In 1926 breakfast had lost not a tittle of its importance. Here in Dorothy L. Sayers's *Clouds of Witness* is Lord Peter Wimsey hearing the news that his brother the Duke of Denver has been arrested on a murder charge: 'Dear me! Well, I suppose one must have one's breakfast.' That breakfast, since Lord Peter was staying in a Paris hotel, was necessarily no more than coffee and rolls. But when Lord Peter arrives at Riddlesdale Lodge, where breakfast is again being served with the Dowager Duchess herself pouring coffee, the scene is very much otherwise.

The Hon. Freddy Arbuthnot is engaged in trying to take the whole skeleton of a bloater out at once ('The very presence of that un-distinguished fish upon the Duchess's breakfast-table indicated a disorganised household') while the detective sent from Scotland Yard is also at the table 'eating curry next to Mr Murbles, the solicitor' consuming a little dry toast. And, worse revelation of all, sausages have failed to appear. 'What,' says Lord Peter, 'Sunday morning in an English family and no sausages? God bless my soul, what's the world coming to?'

But every other meal in the English family's ritual life was almost as important in those days, or in those books. Freeman Wills Crofts again provides a noble example of the importance of lunch. It comes in *Man Overboard* when the sub-sleuth, one Jefferson, is attempting to reconstruct the activities of a suspicious English visitor to Northern Ireland called Platt. Where, he wonders, did Platt have lunch? 'He did not think Platt knew anyone in Hillsborough. Where else could he have had it?' No one, however criminally inclined, could of course forgo that meal. And in what circumstances is Jefferson trying to pin down his man? After tea. Impossible even to think during tea or before. No, it's 'after tea Jefferson lit a pipe and gave himself up to thought'. It is behaviour paralleled by Inspector French in *Anything to Declare?* 'French was impatient to get to his calculations, but it was so nearly supper time that he had to wait till the meal was over.'

Or consider an even more impressive case, R. Austin Freeman's 'inverted' detective story of 1930, *Mr Pottermack's Oversight*, in which Mr P. has decided he will have to murder the man blackmailing him. Here he is in the hours leading up to the deed: 'So the day passed. The mid-day meal was consumed mechanically . . . and dispatched with indecent haste. . . . He lingered over his tea as if he were purposely consuming time, and when at last he rose from the table, he informed Mrs Gadby [his housekeeper] that he had some important work to do and was under no circumstances to be disturbed.' Then, when he has made his final preparations, it is supper time and we read, 'Although he was pretty sharp-set after his strenuous and laborious evening, he made but a hasty meal; for time was precious and he could dispose of the balance of the feast when he had finished his task.' At last, his murder accomplished, 'he sat at the table consuming the arrears of his supper'.

What meals they were, too, those interruptions to the process of detection, or of murder. Inspector Mallett in Cyril Hare's *Death Is No Sportsman*, investigating the case of a man apparently dead of sunstroke - they even had hot summers in the 1930s - cannot proceed without a lunch consisting of trout, illegally poached, followed by 'a steaming steak and kidney pudding'. And Gladys Mitchell's delightful detective, the saurian Mrs Lestrange Bradley, in *Laurels Are Poison* wheedles a young witness with a tea of 'toast, ham, boiled eggs, sardines, new bread, butter, honey and jam'.

E.R. Punshon, in one of his detective stories featuring as investigator (in a somewhat unlikely way) Detective Constable Bobby Owen, has him protecting a threatened tycoon while sharing a meal of 'sole cooked in madeira, roast duck served with green peas done in butter, apple tart with cream, followed by coffee obedient to the maxim of the eastern sage that coffee should be as sweet as love, as black as night, and as hot as hell'. No wonder our young hero failed in his duty and found his charge murdered. But had he perhaps said 'no' to at least that cream we might not have had another classical Golden Age mystery to beat him to the solving.

W.H. Auden.

7 SONGSTERS SINGING

or The Oxblood Book of Detectival Verse

Poetry is not always about the moon in June. Indeed, anything can fire the muse. Even the art of the detective story, odd though that may seem. And I have managed to find seven poems reflecting on the crime story, rigorously excluding mere poems about murders like Browning's 'My Last Duchess'. At one time I nurtured the ambition to collect together enough to fill a whole book. But realism has prevailed.

Detective Story

Who is ever quite without his landscape,
The straggling village street, the house in trees,
All near the church? Or else, the gloomy town-house,
The one with the Corinthian pillars, or
The tiny workmanlike flat, in any case
A home, a centre where the three or four things
That happen to a man do happen?
Who cannot draw the map of his life, shade in
The country station where he meets his loves
And says good-bye continually, mark the spot
Where the body of his happiness was first discovered?

An unknown tramp? A magnate? An enigma always,
With a well-buried past: and when the truth,
The truth about our happiness comes out,
How much it owed to blackmail and philandering.

What follows is habitual. All goes to plan:
The feud between the local common sense
And intuition, that exasperating amateur
Who's always on the spot by chance before us;
All goes to plan, both lying and confession,
Down to the thrilling final chase, the kill.

Yet, on the last page, a lingering doubt:
The verdict, was it just? The judge's nerves,
That clue, that protestation from the gallows,
And our own smile . . . why, yes . . .

But time is always guilty. Someone must pay for
Our loss of happiness, our happiness itself.

W.H. Auden

Don't Guess Let Me Tell You

Personally I don't care whether a detective story writer was educated in night school or in day school

So long as they don't belong to the H.I.B.K. school.

The H.I.B.K. being a device to which too many detective-story writers are prone,

Namely the Had I But Known.

Sometimes it is the Had I But Known what grim secret lurked behind that smiling exterior I would never have set foot within the door,

Sometimes the Had I But Known then what I know now I could have saved at least three lives by revealing to the Inspector the conversation I heard through that fortuitous hole in the floor.

Had-I-But-Known narrators are the ones who hear a stealthy creak at midnight in the tower where the body lies, and, instead of locking their door or arousing the drowsy policeman posted outside their room, sneak off by themselves to the tower and suddenly they hear a breath exhaled behind them,

And they have no time to scream, they know nothing else till the men from the D.A.'s office come in next morning and find them.

Had I But known-ers are quick to assume the prerogatives of the Deity,

For they will suppress evidence that doesn't suit their theories with appalling spontaneity,

And when the killer is finally trapped into a confession by some elaborate device of the Had I But Known-er some hundred pages later than if they hadn't held their knowledge aloof,

Why they say Why Inspector I knew all along it was he but I couldn't tell you, you would have laughed at me unless I had absolute proof.

Would you like a nice detective story for your library which I am sorry to say I didn't rent but owns?

I wouldn't have bought it had I but known it was impregnated with Had I But Knowns.

Ogden Nash

Denouement

All in the library? Then I'll begin.
First reconstruction. Lady Mary,
your story . . .

              No story, but the truth.

Of course. Your truth. You heard
at midnight . . .

                Perhaps later. My truth
is not as precise as grocer's butter.

Just so. Around midnight. . .

                    Not earlier.
Not around because not earlier.

Just so. You heard a sound
like a shot . . .

             a shot like the sound
of a drayman's whip like the flat of a hand
on a naughty buttock like the split of a cane
on a bloodstained thigh.

                Just so.
Did you get that, Sergeant? At midnight,
or just after, and then a thud; you too
Mr Murdo, you heard the thud?

Like the drop of a corpse from a hanging hook,
like a broadbreast turkey on a window tray.

But not the shot?

              I do not listen to shots,
only thuds.

          Just so.
Now Gilchrist the butler . . .

                Gilchrist, you may speak.

Thank you, Lady Mary. I found his Lordship
as I tested the windows; he lay by the sofa.
He had not spilt his whisky though his blood
spoilt the carpet.

            Was there much blood, Gilchrist?

It covered two strange flowers and an Oriental Goddess.
All those arms.

    What did you do then?

I awoke Mr Murdo.

     And you, Mr Murdo?

I awoke Lady Mary.

     And you, Lady Mary?

I awoke.

   And then?

     We all went down
and we looked at the blood. We all took our shoes off
and we danced in the blood. Who would have thought
who would have thought who would have thought

Just so. Thank you all three. Let us pull the curtains.
We must go further into this.

Reginald Hill

The Guilty Party

It is the author who creates the crime
And picks the victim, this blonde dark girl sprawled
Across a bed, stabbed, strangled, poisoned bashed
With a blunt instrument. Or the young middle-aged
Old scandalous and respected beardless greybeard
Destroyed most utterly by some unknown means
In a room with doors and windows 'hermetically sealed'.

So victims and means are found. As for the motive
It is often impersonal, a matter of money,
An estate to be gained, a will cheated on, a secret
Within the family, a discreditable
Business about the building contract for the new school.
It is simple for Hawkshaw, whose life has been
Logically given to the pursuit of logic.
He reads the signs, dustmarks, thumbprint, human and animal blood,
And arrests the solicitor.

                              The author
Puts down his pen. He has but poisoned in jest,
Stabbed and strangled in jest, destroyed in jest
By unknown means the smiling neuter victim.
What has he done that could deserve the tap
Upon the door of his butter-bright smiling room
Where crimes are kept in filing cabinets
Well out of sight and mind, what has he done
To bring this horde of victim villains in,
One paddling fingers in her own bright blood
And staining his face with it, another
Revealing the great wound gaping in his side,
The sliced-up tart carrying a juicy breast,
Inviting him to kiss it: and the villains all
Crowding him with their horrid instruments,
The rope that playfully tightens round his neck,
The blue revolver used to mutilate,
The dagger points to pierce out jelly eyes,
The saw and hammer at their nasty work,
The shapes of agony – and worst of all
The unnamed death that strips away the flesh
And melts the bone, a death unnamable
Yet clearly known.

From all such visions,
Unreal, absurd, phantasmagorical,
We naturally wish to be preserved.
If for a moment this white neutral room
Is filled with smells of rotted or burning flesh
There is a specific by which a respectable
Writer may puff away such nastiness
And regiment like Hawkshaw the unruly
Shapes of life to an ideal order.

He picks up his pen.

Julian Symons

Send for Lord Timothy

The Squire is in his library. He is rather worried.
Lady Constance has been found stabbed in the locked
Blue Room, clutching in her hand
A fragment of an Egyptian papyrus. His degenerate half-brother

Is on his way back from New South Wales,
And what was the butler, Glubb,
Doing in the neolithic stone-circle
Up there on the hill, known to the local rustics
From time immemorial as the Nine Lillywhïte Boys?
The Vicar is curiously learned
In Renaissance toxiocology. A greenish Hottentot,
Armed with a knobkerry, is concealed in the laurel bushes.

Mother Mary Tiresias is in her parlour.
She is rather worried. Sister Mary Josephus
Has been found suffocated in the scriptorium,
Clutching in her hand a somewhat unspeakable
Central American fetish. Why was the little novice,
Sister Agnes, suddenly struck speechless
Walking in the herbarium? The chaplain, Fr O'Goose
Is almost too profoundly read
In the darker aspects of fourth-century neo-Platonism.
An Eskimo, armed with a harpoon
Is lurking in the organ loft.

The Warden of St Phenol's is in his study.
He is rather worried. Professor Ostracoderm
Has been found strangled on one of the Gothic turrets,
Cluthing in his hand a patchouli-scented
Lady's chiffon handkerchief.
The brilliant under-graduate they unjustly sent down
Has transmitted an obscure message in Greek elegiacs
All the way from Tashkent. Whom was the Domestic Bursar
Planning to meet in that evil smelling
Riverside tavern? Why was the Senior Fellow,
Old Doctor Mousebracket, locked in among the incunabula?
An aboriginal Philipino pygmy,
Armed with a blow-pipe and poisoned darts, is hiding behind
The statue of Pallas Athene.

114

A dark cloud of suspicion broods over all. But even now
Lord Timothy Pratincole (the chinless wonder
With a brain like Leonardo's) or Chief Inspector Palefox
(Although a policeman, patently a gentleman,
And with a First in Greats) or that eccentric scholar,
Monsignor Monstrance, alights from the chuffing train,
Has booked a room at the local hostelry
(*The Dragon of Wantley*) and is chatting up Mine Host,
Entirely democratically, noting down
Local rumours and folk-lore.

Now read on. The murderer will be unmasked,
The cloud of guilt dispersed, the church clock stuck at three,
And the year always
Nineteen twenty or thirty something,
Honey for tea, and nothing
Will ever really happen again.

John Heath Stubbs

The Owl Writes a Detective Story

A stately home where doves, in dovecotes, coo,
fields where calm cattle stand and gently moo,
trim lawns where croquet is the thing to do.
This is the ship, the house party's the crew:
Lord Feudal, hunter of the lion and gnu,
whose walls display the heads of not a few,
Her Ladyship, once Ida Fortescue,
who, like his Lordship very highborn too,
surveys the world with a disdainful moue.
Their son—most active with a billiard cue—
Lord Lazy (stays in bed till half past two).
A Balkan Count called Popolesceru
(an ex-Dictator waiting for a coup).
Ann Fenn, most English, modest, straight and true,
a very pretty girl without a sou.
Adrian Finkelstein, a clever Jew.
Tempest Bellairs, a beauty such as you
would only find in books like this (she'd sue
if I displayed *her* to the public view—
enough to say men stick to her like glue).
John Huntingdon, who's only there to woo
(a fact, except for her, the whole house knew)
Ann Fenn. And, last, the witty Cambridge Blue,
the Honourable Algy Playfair, who
shines in detection. His clear 'View halloo!'
puts murderers into a frightful stew.
But now the plot unfolds! What *déjà vu*!
There! In the snow!—The clear print of a shoe!
Tempest is late for her next rendez-vous,
Lord Feudal's blood spreads wide-red sticky goo
on stiff white shirtfront—Lazy's billet-doux
has missed Ann Fenn, and Popolesceru
has left—without a whisper of adieu
or saying goodbye, typical *mauvais gout*!
Adrian Finkelstein, give him his due,
behaves quite well. Excitement is taboo
in this emotionless landowner's zoo.
Algy, with calm that one could misconstrue
(handling with nonchalance bits of vertu)
knows who the murderer is. He has a clue.

But who? But who? Who, who, who, who, who, who?

Gavin Ewart

A Hell of a Writer

Some writers live beyond their age,
Their passing no excuse to mourn,
Their pulse still beating on the page.
The world has cause to celebrate
That day in 1888
When Raymond Chandler was born.

Chicago was his native town,
Though Dulwich College, strange to say,
Was where he gained his cap and gown.
Through Philip Marlowe, private eye –
The Big Sleep and *The Long Goodbye* –
He was to learn that crime *does* pay.

The writer belied the mask he wore,
The raincoat and the soft felt hat.
Married for thirty years and more,
he lived, when Cissy died, in hell
And showed the pulp beneath the shell.
He also loved his Persian cat.

Corruption, his abiding theme,
Was not the game that Marlowe played.
The city could not destroy the dream
Of those unmarked by what they know:
'Down these means streets a man must go . . .
Who is neither tarnished nor afraid.'

Roger Woddis

6 BEGINNINGS

Agatha Christie

Consider Agatha Christie, the most successful writer of detective stories there has ever been, with sales, as has so often been said, exceeded only by the Bible and Shakespeare. How did she begin? What was the first step on the path that led to such renown, such (not to be pussyfoot) riches?

It was a faltering step indeed. Or so it must have seemed at the time. Mrs Christie sent her manuscript of *The Mysterious Affair at Styles* to first one publisher, then another. And another and another and another and another. And only at last after the manuscript had been with the publisher John Lane at the Bodley Head for almost two years (some excuse, in that part of that period came in the last months of World War I) did young Mrs Christie receive a letter one morning asking if she would call at the publishing office 'in connection with the manuscript you have submitted'.

By this time, she says in her charming autobiography, she had actually forgotten the book's existence so busy had she been with her husband's return from the war, with finding and furnishing a London flat and settling in with her baby daughter. At the publishing office genial, but shrewd, John Lane told her that 'some of his readers' had said that the book showed promise, and that, with some changes, it should be publishable.

He then gave young Agatha a lecture about the risks a publisher took in issuing a novel by a new and unknown writer, swiftly pulled an agreement out of his desk drawer and suggested she sign it. It stated she would receive no royalties at all until 2,000 copies had been sold, that half any serial rights would go to the publisher, and that the author was bound to offer him her next five novels, on only

A BIG CITY, A SMALL ROOM

Joe Gores, the only writer to have won Mystery Writers of America Edgar awards in three categories, novel (*A Time of Predators* in 1969), short story and television drama, on leaving Notre Dame University asked his Professor of Creative Writing if he ought to become a writer himself. Professor Sullivan answered: 'It is very simple. Go to a big city and rent a little room with a chair and a table in it. Put your typewriter on the table and your behind on the chair.' Ten years later, the professor finished, 'you'll be a writer.'

Gregory Mcdonald also had advice that led him to crime fiction, from a teacher at school. His admonition went: 'Gentlemen, everyone else will tell you to develop a good memory. I tell you to develop a good forgettory.' From him Mcdonald learnt to suppress, if he could, any ideas he might have. Till the one came along that would not be forgotten, try as he might. So was born *Fletch*, title and hero, investigative journalist, zany character, delightful liar. And in 1975 the book won Mcdonald his first Edgar from the Mystery Writers of America.

Lionel Davidson, too, is a great one for forgetting. He has said that after finishing each of his books (and his first *The Night of Wenceslas* gained him the Crime Writers Association Gold Dagger in Britain in 1961, the first of three) he forgets how to do it. 'Whether,' he says, 'that forgetfulness is of that merciful kind covering things like childbirth or whether because a new book calls for a new method of narration, I've never known.' But, whichever, it leaves poor Lionel beginning again each time. Yet perhaps, since the end results are so dazzling, every author should try to forget every time.

slightly better terms. 'I signed with enthusiasm,' Mrs Christie wrote years later. (Only, note well, publishers, Mrs Christie took her books away from the Bodley Head just as soon as those five novels had been written and she stayed with her next publisher for the rest of her long career.)

And *The Mysterious Affair at Styles* was a book that can be read with pleasure today. It may not be top-notch Christie, but it has in it some of her characteristic sleight-of-hand tricks for delightfully deceiving the reader, and it gave us Hercule Poirot, already replete in all his glory. It did something more, too, something that makes it perhaps easier to understand why those first five publishers failed to realise what they had got in front of their eyes. It was a mystery story in which there was no element of identification with the characters with the possible slight exception of the Watson, dull old Captain

Hastings. It was a book without emotional engagement. It brought to full flower the Golden Age of the pure detective story.

And how had Agatha Christie hit on the key figure of that age, the all-detecting detective? What put Hercule Poirot into her head? Happily, she has told us in that autobiography, though one thing she did not tell us, most likely because it had never emerged from her subconscious, was that Poirot had a sort of precursor. This was the creation of Marie Belloc Lowndes, author of that effective story built round Jack the Ripper, *The Lodger*, and also of *H.R.H. the Prince of Wales: An Account of His Career* (1898). Her detective, retired from the Paris Sûreté and working in London, was called Hercules Popeau.

Another face of Hercule Poirot.

However, Agatha Christie's account of the coming to life of her Hercule Poirot begins with her realising that for the detective story she was contemplating she needed a detective. (It was not her first attempt at writing by any means, even at the age of eleven she had a poem in the Torquay newspaper, 'When first the electric tram did run'.) She went over in her mind, she says, the detectives she had read about, Holmes 'the one and only – I should never be able to emulate *him*', Arsène Lupin (but he was too much a villain), Rouletabille, the young journalist hero of Gaston Leroux's *The Mystery of the Yellow Room*. Here she felt she was getting warmer. What she needed was the sort of person who had not been used before.

She toyed then with having a schoolboy, and realised the difficulties. She toyed with a scientist, and saw she knew nothing of the breed. Then she remembered the Belgian refugees billeted at that stage of World War I on the outskirts of Torquay. 'How about a Belgian police officer?' she thought. And for some reason she decided he ought not to be too young. So she retired him. 'What a mistake I made there,' she cheerfully admits. 'My fictional detective must be well over a hundred by now.'

So she allowed her mind to dwell on such a person. Soon it came to her that he would be excessively tidy, in contrast to her own way with possessions strewn round her bedroom. 'And he should be very brainy.' 'Brainy', delightful word of Agatha Christie's day, somehow expressing admiration mingled with slight distrust. Very English. Then into her mind, she goes on, came the phrase 'little grey cells'. Again, it conveys only a tenuous understanding of mental processes.

Next came the moment of naming, that act essential to firming a character amid the vague swirlings of an author's mind. She hunted for a 'rather grand name – one of those names that Sherlock Holmes and his family had.' Like Mycroft. And into her head there came Hercules. 'He would be a small man – Hercules: a good name.'

She says she does not know how the name Poirot arrived 'whether I saw it in some newspaper or written or something'. No doubt Mrs Belloc Lowndes and her sleuth had sunk deep into her subconscious, if indeed 'Poirot' did spring from 'Popeau'. But when 'Poirot' had come to her she saw that it entailed, somehow, chopping that final 's' off Hercules.

And so it all began, a saga that was to bring the young Agatha fame and fortune to an extraordinary extent, to make her name synonymous with detective fiction the world over.

Simenon

Writing in a notebook he kept, Georges Simenon scrawled, on 25 June 1960, just after he had finished a novel, 'my hundred-eightieth-and-some', a reminiscence of his early childhood. 'From the age of seven or eight,' he wrote, 'I have always been fascinated by paper, pencils, india-rubbers, and a stationer's fascinated me more than a sweetshop or a patisserie.' There we see the very beginnings of a writer.

When he was about eleven, he tells us, he managed at last – his was a poverty-bound childhood – to buy himself a proper notebook, like the ones the students had, not a school exercise-book. In it he set down whatever of others' writings he thought worthy. It was only when he was 15, and on to his second fat notebook, that 'the poetry in it was mine'. At about this time, too, he described to himself a 'corrector of destinies', a figure he thought ought to exist. It was a description he was latter to apply to his Maigret.

Simenon drawn by the Belgian artist
Maurice Vlaminck.

Then, via journalism – he had got into big trouble at his Jesuit school in Liège for editing a mimeographed 'paper' with a caricature on the front of the Principal – he went on to the production, rather than the writing, of commercial short stories, turning them out at an enormous rate. When at the age of 20 he married a painter he agreed to confine himself to this hack fiction so that she could devote herself to art. But every evening, almost in secret, he would write something 'for myself' without any thought of publication.

Eventually he sent some of his more ambitious writing to the famous novelist, Colette, then fiction editor of *Le Matin*. She returned them and returned them again and again when he had revised them. Finally she said to him, 'Look, it is too literary, always too literary.' So he cut out adjectives, adverbs and, as he told an early interviewer for the now famous *Paris Review*, he cut out, too, 'every word which is there just to make an effect'.

In this way there was born that pared-down style which is the envy of all of us writers who try to put things across by splattering adjectives and adverbs on to the pages like painters splodging on the impasto. Simenon gives us instead pencil sketches which, miraculously, convey as much and more. From that advice of

Colette's came what another Francophone crime writer, Thomas Narcejac, has called Simenon's 'nudity of style'.

At last came the day when, feeling his apprenticeship was over and that the pseudonym of 'Sim' could be abandoned, aged now 30, Simenon bought a boat, set out on a canal tour of Holland and wrote, in one sequence within a single year, the first eight Maigret novels. They were a tremendous success, and rightly so, gaining him an enthusiastic write-up in the 'Paris Letter' of the *New Yorker* and translation at once into English, though Simenon himself was to say later that he dared not re-read them since he had devoted only a single day to the revision of each of them.

Yet he always wrote his novels, which are almost all remarkably short, in days rather than weeks or months. Some two days only before he was due to begin one he would pluck from his mind a 'small world' and with it 'a few characters'. Then, in his prime, he would have a medical check-up and, after those two days during which he had made chaotic notes on the back of a manilla envelope, he would begin to write, concentrating with such intensity that after a morning's work he would be totally exhausted, his shirt wringing wet with sweat.

At the end of some 11 or 12 days there would be a new Maigret or a new one of his 'hard' novels, as he called them. And now he would revise for rather longer than one day.

Ngaio Marsh

If some renowned mystery writers took long and long to come to the point of writing with their first book, Ngaio Marsh began the saga of Inspector, later Superintendent, Alleyn in the most casual fashion. A young New Zealander of 35 living with her mother in London in 1933, she was, as she has described in her autobiography *Black Beech and Honeydew*, rather bored one remorselessly rainy Sunday when her mother was temporarily away. 'I read a detective novel from a dim little lending library in Bourne Street,' she says. 'I don't remember the author now, but I think perhaps it was Agatha Christie. I was not a heavy reader in the genre but I had, off and on, turned an idea for a crime story over in my mind.'

And the idea young Ngaio had? (That name is a Maori one from New Zealand, and means either a particular kind of bush, or the way the light falls in a certain manner on water. Your choice. But pronounce it Ni-yo.) It was to take the Murder Game, popular in those days at adult parties – we have become more sophisticated since – and, instead of having the player who has drawn the secret card indicating he must commit a 'murder', pretending to strangle one of the other players, to have a real murder take place. 'I imagine,' she went on modestly to write, 'some round dozen of established practitioners had already discarded this *trouveau* as being too obvious, but I thought it was just fine.' In fact, she has said elsewhere, a French writer had also hit on the idea.

But she knew nothing of that. So she pulled on a mackintosh, took an umbrella, plunged up the basement steps from her flat and 'beat my way through the rain-fractured lamplight' to the shop in Bourne Street, open weekday and Sundays alike. There she bought several penny exercise books, or they may have been twopenny ones – her recollections vary – and some already sharpened pencils. Then it was scribble, scribble, scribble in a whirl of the easy inspiration apt to come to young writers before they realise just how difficult it all is.

She went on, she says, until late that Sunday night. And then, in the evenings she continued to fill those exercise books. Eventually there was a pile of them filled in every line, and then one day she found her mother with her head buried in one of them.

'Is it any good?' she asked. Her mother, she tells us, was no more an addict of the Christie-type story than she was herself. But she did reply 'It's readable.' Then she rubbed her nose and added, 'I couldn't put it down.'

To be frank, in the light of all that has been written in mystery fiction since 1934 when *A Man Lay Dead* was published, the book is one which many readers *will* be able to put down, though with that splendid old tug of 'Who done it?' there all along it is likely they will pick it up again.

Perhaps they will do so not so much for the plot as for the character of the detective young Miss Marsh invented when she got to Chapter Four. Certainly Inspector Alleyn steps ready-made into the ranks of the sleuths of the literature who demand allegiance. This

Ngaio Marsh.

is how readers in the 1930s first saw him, through the eyes of Angela North, part narrator of the book and friend of the young gossip columnist (only 25) who also featured:

> Alleyn did not resemble a plain-clothes policeman she felt sure, nor was he in the romantic manner – white faced and gimlet eyed. He looked like one of her Uncle Hubert's friends, the sort that they knew would 'do' for houseparties. He was very tall and lean, his hair was dark, and his eyes grey, with corners that turned down. They looked as if they would smile easily, but his mouth didn't.

Alleyn came to her, she has said, by the process of conducting a review of all the detectives she had read about. It was a search reminiscent of the one by which Agatha Christie had found Hercule

Poirot. But, having considered all the detectives she could call to mind, including Poirot himself, Ngaio Marsh decided their eccentricities were a little too much of a good thing. Instead, she thought, her 'best chance lay in comparative normality'. She had better not tie any mannerisms, like labels, round the neck of her creation, though she confessed years later looking back that in her early books 'I did not altogether succeed' in this.

At the end of her review, suddenly, Alleyn arrived out of nothing. Since his unusual name is taken from Edward Alleyn – you're meant to pronounce it 'Allen' – the actor of Shakespeare's day and founder at Dulwich College where Ngaio's father had been educated (later to be followed by Raymond Chandler), I think it is fair to guess, however, that this portrait was conceived with him in mind, or in the back of the mind.

Ngaio at the age of six had been so devoted to her father that she once took (in order not to spoil her image of him) the music sheet of a comic song he used occasionally to sing, which with its final line 'A cup of poison lay there by her side' had given her terrible jim-jams, tore it to pieces and buried it in the rubbish heap. Of such childish nightmares are fiction's detectives made.

Michael Innes

It's okay for academics to read detective stories, and even to glory in the vice. There is a nice tale of Dr Wheeler Robinson, one of the great Old Testament scholars, looking over the bookstall at Oxford railway station before a journey and asking the man behind the counter whether he had any other detective stories hidden away since he had read all the ones on display. The man pointed out another display at the other end of the counter. 'Read 'em all.' Stern reply: 'Well, sir, all I can suggest is that you try some serious literature for a change.'

It is less well-looked on in university circles nowadays to write crime fiction. My friend, Cecil Jenkins, a lecturer at the University of Sussex, who was joint winner of the competition for a detective novel written by a don in 1961 with *Message from Sirius* (find a rare copy if you can), subsequently told me he dared not write a successor to it since it would not look good on his CV when he wanted to advance his career. His fellow prizeman, R.J. White, hardly followed up his *The Smartest Grave* either.

However, in the older universities in more remote days even the writing of detective stories was not altogether discouraged. Sir John Masterman, indeed, Vice-Chancellor of Oxford University in the 1950s, had written in 1933 *An Oxford Tragedy*, precursor in a way of the donnish detective story itself. Others, too, had ventured into the limelight of criminous print, Glyn Daniel, Head of the Department of Archaeology at Cambridge, and Mary Fitt, lecturer in Greek at the University College of South Wales from 1919 to 1946, among others in Britain. In America, where they manage matters differently, we have unashamed Amanda Cross, or Professor Carolyn Heilbrun, actually criticising academic life in her erudite and delightful crime stories featuring Professor Kate Fansler.

So in 1936 it was not altogether out of the question for a young academic at Oxford, J.I.M. Stewart, to reflect that, since he spent an enormous amount of time reading detective stories, he might as well supplement his income by writing one. When at the end of a long sea voyage to Australia to take up a post there, he had finished *Death at the President's Lodging*, he did however seek a certain anonymity by calling himself Michael Innes. In America, where they have different sorts of Presidents, they called his book *Seven Suspects*, under which name in paper it has recently filtered back to Britain.

J.I.M. Stewart has written of how he was not, in fact, a very good reader of all the Christies and Queens he devoured. He was happy to wallow in bafflement until the all-cunning author revealed the diabolically clever solution. But, he has said, when it came to producing a crime story of his own he felt duty bound to provide some diabolic cunning himself.

In that part of his task he followed the conventional pattern of the day, and with all the true, beloved complexity. But he also added something new: really donnish talk. It came spouting from the lips even of his police investigator, the new-minted Inspector Appleby, quick as a flash with off-the-cuffs like 'The Deipnosophists . . . Schweighauser's edition . . . Takes up a lot of room . . . Dindorf's compacter.'

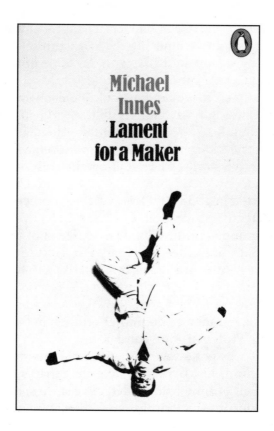

Thus Michael Innes simultaneousıy laid claim to producing fiction at a high level of intelligence while avoiding rising to the high seriousness which he felt, as a student of all that was best in the writings of the centuries, he should not attempt. Later, of course, he did venture on the novel proper, under his own name and initials, and it may be said that his third crime story, *Lament for A Maker* – it followed the splendid *Hamlet, Revenge!* in 1938 – advances a fair way into the territory of the novel which does rather more than set a puzzle and adorn it with trimmings.

But, for some reason, after *Lament for A Maker* Michael Innes backed away from such seriousness in crime and went on simply to give us a dazzling and delightful almost yearly stream of books chronicling, more or less, the rise of Inspector Appleby to the dizzy heights of Commissioner of the Metropolitan Police and a knighthood, and on to retirement jocosities and even the (not altogether successful) fathering of a sleuthish son, Bobby.

On the way he expressed the opinion, in a J.I.M. Stewart novella

'The Man Who Wrote Detective Stories' that the sort of author required in detection was a man who 'loved tumbling out scraps of poetry from a ragbag collection in his mind'. Elsewhere, too, he had made a strong case for the book that sets out to do no more than entertain (and entertain splendidly an Innes does) while he once told me, with how much modest backward exaggeration I do not know, that it had become his habit to produce the new book during the first three weeks of each Long Vacation. *Death at the President's Lodging* took him six long sea-borne weeks, but then it had that fairly fiendish plot.

Raymond Chandler

Fired at 44. Such was the fate of an English-educated, half-Irish American who had, after a somewhat vagabond life, apparently made good in the oil business in California. But Depression days had made things difficult, and Raymond Chandler had also found his home life less happy than it had been now that his wife, older than himself, had reached 60 and was not always well. He had sought relief in secretaries and drink and some of his weekends had lasted till Wednesday. So there he was, with no job, nothing to do and nowhere to go.

His thoughts turned again then to the ambition of his youth when, as he later said himself, 'I wanted to be a writer' though 'that would not have gone down at all, especially with my rich and tyrannical uncle'. He had passively, at the age of 18, agreed to go into the Civil Service in Britain and to study in France and Germany as a preparation.

That ambition to write, however, led him to quit after only six months the position in the Admiralty he eventually gained, third out of 600 in the competitive exam, and to take up occasional journalism, including the penning of verses, 'most of which', he wrote to his British publisher, Hamish Hamilton, in 1950, 'now

THE CASE OF THE
WANDERING CARBUNCLE

Raymond Chandler's London solicitor in his latter years was Michael Gilbert, fellow crime novelist. Mr Gilbert drew up Chandler's will, and was also the recipient in 1955 of a letter from his client recounting how unpleasant he had found a voyage back to America from England. 'Still practising to be a non-drinker,' Chandler wrote, '(and it's going to take a damn sight more practising than I have time for) I sat alone at a table in the corner and refused to have anything to do with the other passengers.'

Michael Gilbert's ambition to be writer of crime stories as well as a lawyer was boosted while he was a prisoner-of-war in Italy and read – one of the few crime books available – Cyril Hare's excellent legal detective story *Tragedy-at-Law*. After gaining freedom from his camp when Italy surrendered and eventually rejoining his regiment, Mr Gilbert, back in civilian life, re-wrote his first book, *Close Quarters*, started in 1930 inspired by Hare.

Later, in 1952, he drew on his prisoner-of-war experiences to write *Death in Captivity* (called *The Danger Within* in America), surely the only whodunit to be set in a prisoner-of-war camp. And, yet later in 1985, he used his post-escape wanderings in the Italian countryside for *The Long Journey Home*, though its hero is a man who in post-war days has embarked on a long contemplative holiday in the Apennines.

Curiously, Mr Gilbert's own Apennine experiences dodging the still active German forces have been recorded by two other writers, his fellow escapees in 1943. Eric Newby, the distinguished author of travel books, wrote of those days in *Love and War in the Apennines*, and Tony Davies called his account of making their way towards the Allied Forces slowly pushing their way up Italy, *When the Moon Rises*. But there is one difference in the two tales. Each author speaks of the very painful carbuncle which added unpleasantly to Michael Gilbert's troubles. Newby places this excrescence on Gilbert's behind: Davies puts it under an armpit. Inevitably to mind comes Dr John H. Watson's wandering wound located at different times by Conan Doyle and perhaps the most charming of the Holmes tales, 'The Blue Carbuncle', though that is about the garnet-like gem rather than the painful boil-like inflammation.

seem to me deplorable, but not all'. Journalism, however, paid little, and young Chandler returned to the United States where he had been born, toying with writing only to the extent of 'almost' selling to the *Atlantic* a Henry James pastiche.

But now, wandering up and down the Pacific coast by car wondering what to do, he began to read pulp magazines 'because', as he eventually wrote to Hamish Hamilton, 'they were cheap to throw away and because I never had at any time any taste for the kind of thing which is known as women's magazines'. It struck him, he says, that some of the writing in such magazines as *Black Mask*, in which Dashiell Hammett and Erle Stanley Gardner were appearing, was 'pretty forceful and honest'.

He decided that trying to contribute stories of the sort *Black Mask* was using, the 'hard-boiled' detective tale, might be a good way to learn to write fiction 'and get paid a small amount of money at the same time'. To teach himself, he adapted the method that he had had to undergo as a schoolboy at Dulwich College, translating from Latin into English and then after a while translating back into Latin. Now he spent hours reducing *Black Mask* stories to their bare bones and then rewriting them in his own words. 'It would seem that a classical education might be a rather poor basis for writing novels in a hard-boiled vernacular,' he said after he had achieved his success. 'I happen to think otherwise.'

With five months' work he produced, and sold, a long short story called 'Blackmailers Don't Shoot' and, he wrote, 'after that I never looked back, although I had a good many uneasy periods looking forward'. Cannabalising two stories he had had in *Black Mask*, 'Killer in the Rain' which had appeared in the January 1935 issue and 'The Curtain' from the September 1936 issue, he had inside three months written the first of the Philip Marlowe novels, *The Big Sleep*. (The seeming argot expression for death was his own invention, though philologists later annexed it to genuine underworld talk.)

Chandler took eleven of the book's chapters from 'Killer' and ten from 'The Curtain' adding eleven others new. But each of the chapters he 'borrowed' from the short stories contains many parts and paragraphs that he considerably extended. And the killer in *The Big Sleep*, Carmen Sternwood, she of the 'little sharp predatory teeth, white as fresh orange pith', is a femaled (what a word) version of Dade Trevillyan, the psychopath murderer of 'The Curtain', passed through the character of Carmen Dravec, of 'Killer'. There are 21 characters in the novel, if you count. Four of them are composites from the two short stories, four were completely new and the remaining 13 come almost equally from each story.

In much the same way Marlowe himself grew up through Chandler's *Black Mask* stories, in which the detective figure is at first not named at all in 'Killer', becomes Carmady with no forename in the three *Mask* stories that followed and then in the next three gets John in front of Dalmas, until in the first words of *The Big Sleep* he steps into full life, Chandler's wife having persuaded him out of the 'Mallory' in his early drafts. (Both names with their references to English literature underline the knight-errantry lurking in the seedy California office.)

So at last Philip Marlowe came to life, with 'the fire and the dash necessary for vivid writing' (Chandler's words to Philip Morgan, associate editor of the *Atlantic*, commenting adversely on the puzzle-maker's mind), in those very first words:

> It was about eleven o'clock in the morning, mid October, with the sun not shining and a look of hard wet rain in the clearness of the foothills. I was wearing my powder-blue suit, with dark blue shirt, tie and display handkerchief, black brogues, black wool socks with dark blue clocks on them. I was neat, clean, shaved and sober, and I didn't care who knew it.

The words, with their hint of self-mockery, have an air of utter rightness, of being the only possible ones there could be. A crime classic had been born.

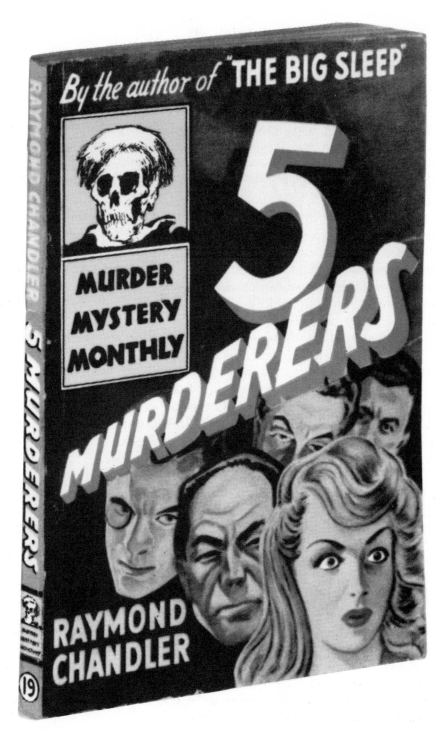

Ross Macdonald

Some writers begin with a bang; others whimper their way to what it is they want to do. Ross Macdonald, who at his peak was one of the very few writers simultaneously on the bestseller lists and taught on literature courses in colleges all across America, came up the whimper way.

Born in Canada in 1915, he and his mother were deserted by his sea-captain father and left in sad financial straits. Yet, highly intelligent, he had aspirations to take a place in middle-class society and succeeded in getting to college and even, in 1941, going to California, which his American mother had always told him should be his spiritual home, to work for a doctorate in English Literature. All this was, in a way, his first step towards the writing for which eventually he became famous. Indeed, his first title for the book with which he established himself, *The Galton Case*, was 'The Castle and the Poorhouse'.

But before he came to that he had other, more tentative fiction to produce. While serving in the US Navy between 1943 and 1945 he wrote a first crime novel, *The Dark Tunnel*, under his own name, Kenneth Millar. Its hero was a private eye called Chet Gordon, who was to feature in one more book, *Trouble Follows Me*.

Despite his erudite literary education, Macdonald found that mystery fiction was somehow the only mode he could write in. 'My one attempt to write a regular autobiographical novel,' he once said, 'turned out so badly that I never showed it to my publisher and I left the manuscript, I think, in an abandoned blacking factory.' Somewhat obscure joke, paying tribute as a literary ancestor (failed) to Charles Dickens and his unhappy boyhood days in the blacking factory by Hungerford Stairs on the Thames.

So much for the negative reason for turning to crime. On the positive side was the fact that the books of Dashiell Hammett and Raymond Chandler seemed to Kenneth Millar to achieve 'a popular and democratic literature' with their heroes continuing in an urban setting the masculine and egalitarian traditions of frontier America. He felt, too, that there was more to be done with the 'hard-boiled' style than even these masters had achieved.

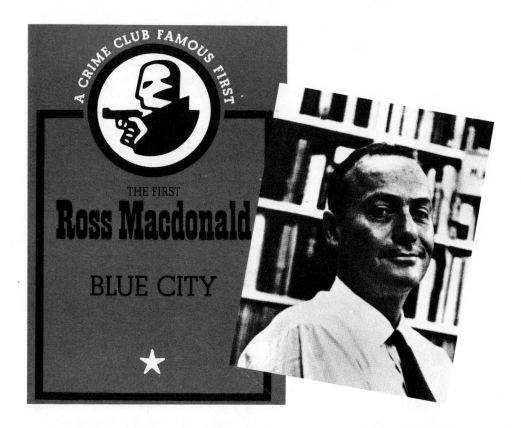

So, Navy service done, he wrote 'in a kind of angry rapture' first *Blue City*, still as Kenneth Millar, and then *The Three Roads* (heavy literary reference here to the *Oedipus Tyrannus* of Sophocles, of which more later). Then in 1949 he wrote *The Moving Target*, the first of his novels with Lew Archer as its hero (or in the first British edition, for some unknown reason, Lew Arless; and later, of course, in the movies Archer became Harper, because Paul Newman always had to play heroes beginning with 'H').

For *The Moving Target* Millar adopted, perhaps as a way of distancing himself from the autobiographical millstone that had put his plain novel into the blacking factory or because his wife, Margaret, was already published as Margaret Millar, the name John Macdonald – only to find himself confused with John D. MacDonald, busy producing the Travis McGee books. So he was forced to become in succession John Ross Macdonald and finally plain Ross Macdonald. His wife, the splendid suspense novelist, has always retained the name Margaret Millar.

Seven Lew Archer books followed, each one by and large an advance on the one before. But it was not until *The Galton Case* in 1959 that Macdonald felt he had really cracked it. In a fairly confessional essay called 'Writing *The Galton Case*' he has told what he felt himself at last able to do. 'In the red spiral notebook where I set down my first notes,' he writes, 'Oedipus made an appropriately early appearance.' The Greek king of old, who gave Freud the name of the complex that goes with a suppressed desire to murder one's father, was appropriate because now at last Kenneth Millar was on the point of being able to write about murders in the buried pasts of his characters and that disappearing sea-captain was being put in his place.

Dozens of ideas, Macdonald says, were going through his mind at that time. But they lacked at first an organising principle. Then a variation on the Oedipus story gave him what he wanted. 'It appears,' he writes, 'in the notebook briefly and abruptly without preparation: Oedipus angry vs. parents for sending him away to a foreign country.' He himself, he says, had been haunted for years by an imaginary boy who, he realised, was the darker side of his own boyhood, 'by his sixteenth year he had lived in fifty houses and committed the sin of poverty in each of them'. That boy becomes the central figure of the book.

But there were false starts even yet; the whimpers were not over. Each start began the story where in the final version it was to end. In the first the boy is the narrator, and his experiences follow fairly closely Kenneth Millar's own. This attempt, Macdonald says, 'died in mid-sentence on its thirteenth page'. Changing the boy's name from Tom to Willie, Macdonald had another go with his youthful hero, less himself now, as narrator. This got further, but again ran into the sand. Only when Macdonald brought to the book his narrator of old, Archer, did he really get going.

Archer, too, of course, is a kind of self-portrait. Macdonald tells an amusing story about this. He was invited, he says, to lunch by a television producer who was contemplating a series with Archer. The producer asked if Archer was based on anybody. 'Yes,' I said. 'Myself.' Then, he goes on, the producer 'gave me a semi-pitying Hollywood look' and, despite hastily adding that he had known real detectives and watched them at work, Macdonald knew that the project had foundered at that moment.

But, even with the discovery that Archer ('I wasn't Archer exactly, but Archer was me') was the right narrator for *The Galton Case*,

Macdonald was not out of trouble. When he was near the end of the first full draft, he says, 'I got morally tired and lost my grip on my subject, ending the book (which at that stage was called *The Enormous Detour*) with a dying fall.' Happily, he had a friend who was able to remind him 'that a book like mine could not succeed as a novel unless it succeeded in its own terms as a detective novel'. He went back to the ending he had had for his second version, and *The Galton Case* came to life and thereafter the work of Ross Macdonald achieved the high status in crime-writing acknowledged by the English departments of colleges and readers by the hundred thousand.

5 FAVOURITES

The Moonstone

T.S. Eliot, that great reader of detective stories who once incorporated some lines from the Holmes story 'The Musgrave Ritual' into his play about Thomas à Becket, *Murder in the Cathedral*, in introducing the World's Classics edition of Wilkie Collins's *The Moonstone* called it 'the first, the longest and the best of modern English detective stories'. It is a panegyric that could be challenged. But certainly *The Moonstone* was the first work in English fiction to show at full length a detective detecting, that delicious character, Sergeant Cuff, at work.

Its originality perhaps accounts for the tepid critical reaction the book got in 1868 when it was transferred from Dickens's magazine *All the Year Round* to volume form. The *Pall Mall Gazette* for example could rise to nothing higher than 'in sliding-panels, trap-doors and artificial beards Mr Collins is nearly as clever as anyone who has ever fried a pancake in a hat'. But the public loved it, and Collins at one time was earning as a writer as much as £10,000 a year, which is comparable to the salary the head of a major industrial company might receive today.

Into *The Moonstone* Collins put much that was to become a staple of detective novels down the years. There is the innocent man who must prove despite all the evidence that he did not commit the crime. There is Sergeant Cuff's remark, since repeated ten thousand times, 'the pieces of the puzzle are not all put together yet'. There is his 'In all my experience along the dirtiest ways of this dirty little world, I have never met with such a thing as a trifle yet', combining in one sentence the essences of Holmes and, surely, Philip Marlowe. There is Cuff's throwaway, mysterious remarks like 'Nobody has stolen the Diamond'. Poirot living before his time.

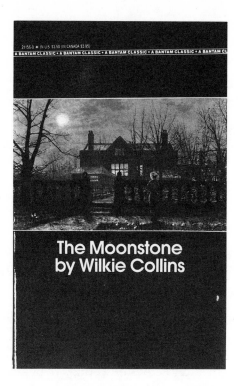

As to *The Moonstone* being the best, it is in fact not possible even in reverse to settle, as Dr Johnson once said, 'the point of precedency between a louse and a flea'. But there is much that is magnificent in the book, right up to its splendidly unexpected solution to the mysterious theft of that haunting diamond, the Moonstone, itself. And Collins slipped in his clues to that in as fair-play a manner as Dorothy L. Sayers at her cricketing best, complete with as juicy a box of red herrings as you could wish.

Yet perhaps one should admit that *The Moonstone* is at least as much a novel proper as it is a detective story. It is full of fine and deep character studies. Each of its various narrators is a person plumbed to the bottom, or as nearly so as Victorian taboos would allow (and there are hints that sneak past some of those). Rachel Verinder, the heroine, is, for instance, convincingly shown as a 'good' girl – even Dickens had trouble doing that – and yet is no namby-pamby and is shown to us clearly and well as being altogether in love.

And running through and through the whole long book is a theme, worthy of the highest attention, the irrational that lies waiting and ominous just below the apparently rational surface of society. The irrational is present at the core, in that gem the Moonstone itself, worshipped in India under the shifting light of the moon, appearing when looked at 'unfathomable'. It is present, powerfully, in the Shivering Sands that lie close to Lady Verinder's comfortable house, a quicksand 'glittering with a golden brightness' that hides 'the horror of its false brown face'. It is there in a hundred glanced-at details, like Franklin's wild perturbation, when he learns the truth, contrasted with 'that strictly logical consistency of conduct which distinguished every man and woman who may read these lines in every emergency of their lives'.

Against his symbols of the irrational, Collins set symbols, as telling, of what he called the Actual. The fabulous Moonstone, it is pointed out, is 'mere carbon'. Old Betteredge, the house steward, says of the painter whose designs Franklin and Rachel are copying, 'the one, I mean, who stocked the world with Virgin Marys, and had a sweetheart at the baker's'. And Collins delighted to put in ironic references one after another to 'the nineteenth century . . . the age of progress'.

This presence of the irrational, the ungovernable, lurking in wait is still a nightmare for twentieth-century readers, and its presence in *The Moonstone* makes it much more for us than a mere story of detection. It was as secretly affecting to its first audience as well. The Victorian Age was marked as much as anything by its struggle to deny and conceal all signs of the uncontrollable, from the dog-eat-dog life of the slums hidden behind its tall and imposing buildings to the realities of sexual relations. The *Westminster Review* had already complained of Collins's novel *Basil* that it dwelt 'on details of the sexual appetite', which by today's standards, of course, it hardly did. But Collins certainly wanted to twitch aside that veil where he could, as he does in just five words of the letter left behind by the crippled maidservant who has fallen violently in love with Franklin Blake, across the class barrier. If he will say one kind thing about her, she writes, her ghost will hear it 'and tremble with the pleasure'.

The psychoanalyst Charles Ryecroft, who made a particular study of *The Moonstone*, postulates that the yellow diamond itself, with its central flaw and ever-changing lustre, is a symbol of the female (feminists, don't read on) and that its theft represents a defiance of the prohibited intercourse between Franklin and Rachel. The fact of the stone not being seen after the theft is the equivalent, he goes on, to the convention of Victorian days that women knew nothing about the sexual act – 'Shut your eyes and think of England'. Rachel's insincere denial that she has any knowledge of the theft, then, is a symbol of the actual hollowness of that convention.

Seen from the masculine point of view, Charles Ryecroft argued, the theft of the Moonstone was the symbolic act of Franklin's un-admitted wish to have the same sort of sexual relationship with Rachel as he has had with women of a lower class before. He goes on to draw a parallel between Franklin, the good lover, and Rachel's other cousin, Geoffrey Abelwhite, the hypocritical bad lover, who eventually managed to acquire the Moonstone and is murdered for it. He suggests, in short, that the theme of the book (I would say *one* theme of the book) is an unconscious representation of the sexual act, with its four main characters, Franklin and Ablewhite, Rachel and her crippled maid, Roseanna, representing different aspects of a society which had created two opposed ideas of women, as beings of total purity and as persons degraded and sexual.

The theory seems to me to hold together, though I think it is one aspect only of the long and complex book. If it is there, then with its direct reference to that powerful emotion of sexuality it probably accounts for the tugging underlying power the book has. Yet it should not be forgotten, too, that it is a splendid detective story, full of suspense, rich in hidden clues, shot on occasion with humour, a classic of crime.

The Hound of the Baskervilles

I suppose if you tried hard enough you could come across English-speaking people who have never heard of *The Hound of the Basker-villes*. But, if they were any sort of reader, filmgoer or TV watcher, you would be almost certain to get some response to the thought of the huge terrifying dog pursuing an innocent across a dark landscape. Yet that image, wonderfully powerful though it is, is not, I believe, what lies at the heart of Conan Doyle's novel. It is not what accounts, fundamentally, for its success. What lies at

OUT OF THE PAGES INTO THE CESSPOOL

One of the penalties of being an author of crime fiction is being called on to solve crimes in real life. Erle Stanley Gardner, a lawyer himself before he turned to Perry Masonry, founded in 1948 a Court of Last Resort, a group of lawyers who took up cases considered to be hopeless. A good many of them they won. Edgar Allen Poe, on the other hand, who took it upon himself to 'solve' the mysterious death of Mary Rogers in New York in 1841 by writing a story 'The Mystery of Marie Roget' set in Paris, was not really successful.

Conan Doyle, however, did have triumphs in the world of real crime. In 1906 he rook up the case of the son of a Parsi clergyman of the Church of England, one George Edalji, who had been convicted of maiming horses and sentenced to seven years. Doyle visited the scene, made many enquiries, drew conclusions and succeeded in showing the conviction was unjust to the point of getting young Edalji released. At that time there was no Court of Criminal Appeal and so Doyle failed to get Edalji's sentence formally annulled, but the affair did help bring about the institution of such a court.

In a second case Doyle's intervention was as successful but much delayed. Oscar Slater, a petty criminal who had been sentenced to life imprisonment for murder on highly dubious identification evidence, contrived after he had been in gaol for 15 years to get an appeal through to the creator of Sherlock Holmes. Doyle backed the efforts of others and paid out good money, and, after 18 years in prison, Slater was freed 'for good conduct'. Doyle's comment: 'What a cesspool it all is!'

its heart is fear, not of a gigantic hound, but of something within each of us ourselves.

When in 1894 Doyle came to write *The Hound of the Baskervilles*, Sherlock Holmes had been 'dead' for eight years. Doyle, longing to do more serious things in English fiction, had sent this incubus ever crouched on his shoulders tumbling over the Reichenbach Falls locked in the arms of the evil Professor Moriarty. An outcry had followed. Processions of young men marched on the offices of the

Basil Rathbone – most famous of film 'Holmeses'.

146

Strand Magazine in London determined to be told it wasn't true, that their hero was still at work. In America 'Let's Keep Holmes Alive' clubs were formed. Doyle weathered that first outburst. But the pressure never greatly slackened, and in the back of his mind, too, we may suspect, he half-wanted to write more about his dual *alter egos*, Holmes and Watson.

So when on a golfing holiday in Norfolk with his friend Fletcher Robinson, it rained all day and they fell to talking first about the local legend of the giant ghost-dog called the Black Shuck and then about a similar tale told of Dartmoor, Sherlock Holmes threw off the great slab of stone his creator had buried him beneath. To a publisher who had offered a very large sum Doyle sent a postcard (typical modest immodesty) saying simply 'Yes. A.C.D.'

With Fletcher Robinson, Doyle visited Dartmoor, was driven over it by a coachman named Baskerville, went to see the dreaded prison and learnt that one of the most brutal warders there was a man called Selden – a name he was to give to his escaped convict. He began to think that he needed for the tale forming in his mind somewhere less cosy than Brook Manor on the edge of the Moor from which the original wicked squire had chased his wife and had been killed, so legend said, by her faithful hound, now turned into a ghost. Here, too, Doyle would have seen the granite slab that rests on wicked Sir Richard's tomb, put there, they say, to keep him safely in.

So, looking for a grimmer mansion, Doyle then remembered his feelings of apprehension on arriving as a boy at Stonyhurst, the isolated boarding school in Lancashire he was sent to. From Stony-hurst, too, he was soon to take another element in the tale, a long, dark alley, down which the younger boys would dare each other to go. Out of it he made 'the famous Yew Alley of Baskerville Hall' with at its end one night 'the footprints of a gigantic hound'. In the finished book he placed his invented Hall 14 miles distant from Dartmoor Prison, where in fact it would have been somewhere in the smiling Devon countryside. But poetic licence has its rights. 'I have never been nervous about details,' Doyle once said. And quite right too.

Thus he gathered together the elements of what might have been no more than a somewhat romanticised tale with behind it a case for a revived Sherlock Holmes to solve. He had yet to devise a way for his hero to survive the Reichenbach and he made his story take place before the great detective had encountered Moriarty.

But out of the working of a true writer's mind there was to emerge

before pen was set to paper, or perhaps even as it was sent flying over
the unsullied pages, an antagonist yet more formidable than the evil
professor. This was Nature, brute Nature. It is a force within ourselves that we still, if we let ourselves think, view with dread, the
rising up of impulses and desires clean contrary to the decent usages
of civilisation. It was something that the Victorians, who thought
Man had conquered the primitive and was firmly on the road of
Progress, particularly dreaded. The word they used for it was the
'atavistic'.

The story of *The Hound of the Baskervilles* is strewn with references
to atavism. We get them even in its first splendid dialogue when
Holmes in his absolutely best form teases unmercifully poor, stolid
Watson in asking him to make deductions from a walking-stick, a
'Penang lawyer'. To prove his point, Holmes looks up the name of
the visitor who had carelessly left the stick behind in the *Medical
Directory*. He finds Dr James Mortimer, of Grimpen, Dartmoor, is
author of a *Lancet* article 'Some Freaks of Atavism' and of 'Do We
Progress?' in the *Journal of Psychology*.

Then when Watson has escorted down to Dartmoor the new heir
to Baskerville Hall and they have caught a glimpse of the escaped
convict, Selden, the Notting Hill murderer (that soubriquet always
gives me an extra pleasure that I have made my home in that part of
London), they see a face 'all seamed and scored with vile passions',
one that might have belonged to 'one of those old savages who dwelt
in the burrows on the hillsides'. And it is in one such ancient cave
that a mysterious stranger (guess who) shortly proves to have set
up camp, thus once more drawing our attention to the primitive
that lurks.

Finally, it is Sherlock Holmes's ability to use his eyes 'trained to
examine faces and not their trimmings', that gives him the clue that
a portrait of the wicked Sir Hugo Baskerville, original cause of the
Hound legend, in fact resembles the apparent newcomer to the
district who proves to be the would-be murderer of the innocent Sir
Henry Baskerville. (I give nothing away, though I suspect anyone
who makes an effort of recollection will know who the villain was.)
The fellow, Holmes says in summing-up, is 'a throwback' to the evil
original.

So, Doyle superimposed this extra dimension onto a tale about
a huge hound chasing a rich young heir across the dangerous,
quagmire-thick moor. (In fact, none of Dartmoor's bogs is anything like as capable of swallowing up a villain as Doyle made his

imaginary Grimpen Mire – more permissible poetic licence.) It touches because of this a chord deep buried in all of us, our fear of what we might be capable of doing. And thus there was made out of a simple detection story a book it is impossible to forget.

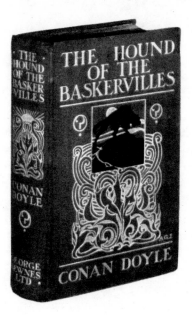

The Maltese Falcon

It is for its picture of the private eye as he ought to be that I most cherish *The Maltese Falcon*. Sam Spade is that admirably indepen-dent figure who, as Raymond Chandler famously said, is 'not himself mean' though he has to go down 'these mean streets'. Hammett describes Spade at the very start of the book as 'a blond satan'. A satan he is, no namby-pamby, streetwise, capable even of actions not everyone would approve.

Somerset Maugham once denigrated him uncompromisingly as 'a nasty piece of goods' and as 'an unscrupulous rogue and heartless

ON THE OTHER SIDE

Not all crime writers have always been on the side of the angels. There's a good handful who unashamedly include in what is called in India their 'bio-data' the fact that they have been in gaol.

Foremost among them as a writer is Chester Himes, author of the splendidly lively and macabre stories about the Harlem detectives, Coffin Ed Johnson and Grave Digger Jones. It was while serving a seven-year term in Ohio State Penitentiary that Himes, after reading some Hammett, conceived the notion of writing crime 'like it is'.

Another man who served almost as long a term in the pen is Donald Gaines. He created Kenyatta, black revolutionary, hero of a series of books that were violent and sexually explicit ahead of their time. Gaines had been a numbers runner, a thief and a bootlegger.

Less violent (and a much smoother writer) is Donald MacKenzie, a Canadian who sets his books mostly in London, many featuring John Raven, discredited Scotland Yard man. MacKenzie has described his life as going from playboy to professional thief, to prison inmate to self-employed author. There is a lot of authenticity in the pages.

Far fewer books were written by another self-confessed burglar, O.J. Currington, whose *A Bad Night's Work*, published in London in 1974, graphically described what it feels like to break and enter. I well remember how, when I was escorting a party of American crime fans – mostly ladies – round Britain Mr Currington held them enthralled far into the night with his stories of committing real crime.

He wrote *A Bad Night's Work* while serving his second, and last term, mostly at night in what had once been the prison's 'hanging cell'. A friendly warder stuck to the 'lights out' rule but turned a blind eye to candlelight. However, making the story 'as near authentic as I dared' earned the disapproval of the authorities. So he made a copy on paper appropriated from the prison office and smuggled it out.

crook'. Roy Cohn, Senator McCarthy's hatchet-man in the 1960s, had *The Maltese Falcon* banned from US Information Service Libraries not only, one guesses, because Hammett was a Communist party member but also because the book showed as a hero a man not entirely admirable. But if Spade was a satan, he was, note, a blond satan. White. Ultimately he is a good man, and a moral one. He cannot be called a white witch, but he is a white wizard.

He is a man free from the clinging things that prevent most of us from always doing what is ultimately right. He is free from the lure of money, happy in that tacky office where 'a half-curtained window, eight or twelve inches open, let in from the court a current of air faintly scented with ammonia'. This, indeed, was Hammett's legacy to his legion of successors, providing them with an essential of their way of life, what the critic James Sandoe once vividly called 'a sense of used paper cups'.

Spade is free, too, from sentiment. At the end of the book when he has tracked down the stunningly attractive Brigid O'Shaughnessy as the murderer of his partner she tries to appeal to his softer feelings. But, though he looks at her 'hungrily from her hair to her feet and up to her eyes again', he says, 'I won't play the sap for you.'

And he is free from something even more dragging down than the sexual urge. He is free from the fear of death. At a climax of the case he tells Brigid a long story, which she altogether fails to see the point of. But what he is saying is just this, that in the end he will do what he has to do, even if it brings him death. Or, as he puts it when threatened later with torture, 'I'll make it a matter of your having to call it off or kill me.'

The story he tells is about one Flitcraft, a man he was once hired to find after he had mysteriously gone missing for no apparent reason. He discovered, he tells Brigid, that on his way to lunch one day, a day no different from any other, Flitcraft was passing a construction site when a heavy steel beam fell from the eighth or tenth floor and smacked the sidewalk next to him. 'He was more shocked really than frightened,' he says. 'He felt like somebody had taken the lid off life and let him look at the works.' And when Flitcraft had seen what life was really like, something beyond any ultimate controlling, he just went off into the blue.

Ironically, in fact, Spade's story goes, Flitcraft before long set himself up another life with just the same appearance of order in it, right down to a second wife like his first, 'the kind of women that play games of golf and bridge and like new salad recipes'. But Spade himself is immune from that failing. He remembers always that he is at the mercy of chance, and this frees him from the trammels of life.

In his freedom from the blinkers which we ordinary mortals clamp so eagerly on to our eyes ('Always keep a-hold of Nurse for fear of finding something worse', as the poet Belloc put it) Spade is, no matter how mean the streets he goes down, the Great Detective. He is not bound, as most of us are, by the portrait we have made of ourselves or by a limited pre-ordained attitude we take to life's unexpectednesses.

The people that Spade comes across in his hunt for the killer of his distinctly imperfect partner, Archer, are so bound. There is the arch-villain Gutman (as well named as Conan Doyle's villains, if a little more obviously, with that suggestion of gobbling greed) who seems only to think the way to deal with life is to eat up everything in his path. 'If you lose a son,' he says when Spade suggests he sends his favoured gunsel ('I feel towards Wilmer just exactly as if he were my own son') as a fall-guy to the police, 'by Gad, if you lose a son it's possible to get another, there's only one Maltese Falcon.' So that reputedly enormously valuable statuette seduces him, as it cannot seduce Spade.

Dashiell Hammett and a magazine idea of his Sam Spade.

Equally Spade is contrasted with the homosexual Joel Cairo, a figure solely of inward-turned self-love, and with Brigid herself, fixed as a pathological liar, changing the version of herself she presents as casually as she changes clothes, hardly even giving herself the same name twice. But Spade's self-image is never so rigid. Flitcraft reminds him.

But the Great Detective, and 'hard-boiled' Sam Spade is just as much such as Sherlock Holmes himself, is one who is capable of breaking out of moulds such as those he meets have placed round themselves. Spade sees life as it is, and he is as well capable, like Holmes, of putting himself soul and body into the minds of others.

At the end of the book he accuses Brigid of killing Archer by making him 'lick his lips and go with her grinning from ear to ear', an accusation based on a pure clue worthy of Dame Agatha Christie herself, put squarely before us in Chapter Two, 'Death in the Fog' (a classical chapter heading, to boot), yet disguised with splendid neatness. Brigid then asks him, 'How did you know he – he licked his lips and looked –?' Spade knew because he could jump into another's mind. And, in doing so, he shows that such a sympathy for our fellow human beings is what we, too, ought to attempt. He is a true hero, an exemplar.

The Talented Mr Ripley

Patricia Highsmith's opening words for *The Talented Mr Ripley* are: 'Tom glanced behind him.' At once we are plunged into a world she made her own. No elaborate explanation of who this 'Tom' is, what his forename is, what he looks like. No, we are in a floating world where the creature called Tom swims into our ken. And, equally, 'glanced behind him' immediately gives us a feeling of unease. And it is for her picture of our world as a place of unease, of suddennesses, of chance working this way and that willy-nilly in *The Talented Mr Ripley*, together with the three other novels that brought us Tom's life, that we stand deeply in Miss Highsmith's debt.

Let me quote the next few words of the book, only noting before I do so that in a little work called *Plotting and Writing Suspense Fiction*, written in 1966, Patricia Highsmith advised would-be writers to begin always with some tiny riddle, something to make the reader ask a question. How cunningly in even her first four words here does she do that. And then, as the question they summon up begins to be answered, with equal cunning she tickles us with other tiny riddles demanding answers.

'. . . and saw a man coming out of the Green Cage, heading his way. Tom walked faster. There was no doubt the man was after him. Tom had noticed him five minutes ago, eyeing him carefully from a table, as if he weren't quite sure, but almost.' In those last five words we get another aspect of the ever-shifting world of Patricia Highsmith, which is our world very much of today laid bare for us. It is the wibble-wobble uncertainty of things. The man is not quite sure. But he is almost sure. He is perched on a narrow bar. He could topple over either way. In her later novel *A Tremor of Forgery* Patricia Highsmith hits off a tiny phrase which encapsulates all that uncertainty: 'it was a brinkish decision'.

Tom, too, in the opening page or two of *The Talented Mr Ripley* makes a brinkish decision. Should he hide with a fair chance of safety from his mysterious pursuer in a dark doorway, or should he go into a bar where it is terribly likely the man will follow him? He chooses, of course, the riskier alternative. He is an inhabitant of the world of risks, and for our guidance he swims with its currents.

He turns out to have won the bet with himself, with life's hazards. His pursuer only wants him to contact his son, Tom's friend, who has gone to Europe and gone to ground there. It is a piece of great luck for Tom who is in a financial jam and something of an illegal one, too. 'Something always turned up,' his creator writes. 'That was Tom's philosophy.' The reference to Dickens's Mr Micawber stands out a mile. But there is a significant difference between the two fictional beings. Dickens, though he delights in Micawber, feels bound to disapprove of him until he has brought about a fairly unlikely metamorphosis in Australia. Patricia Highsmith delights in Tom as he is, amoral and before too long in the book a murderer and a murderer who does not repent.

Dickens lived in a world where, outwardly at least, if you did wrong you were expected both to feel a sense of guilt and to pay in due course a proper penalty. In Tom Ripley's universe you do not

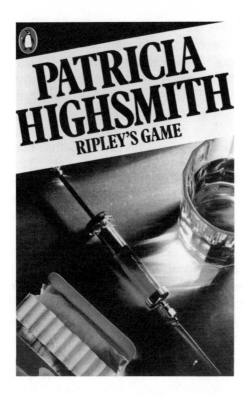

pay the penalty and neither do you feel the weight of that sense of guilt which has been passed down to us through the ages.

In *The Talented Mr Ripley* Tom is, of course, only just entering the universe he is to make his own. In the book's early pages he, like us, is affected by that feeling of guilt. It is only, in fact, when he commits the crime we think of as bringing down most guilt on our heads, murder, that paradoxically he begins to free himself from the burden and his crimes come to seem to us, to quote the critic Maurice Richardson, 'almost graceful, like the swinging antics of a gibbon in the jungle'. At the end of the third Ripley book, *Ripley's Game*, he comes face to face with the widow of a man he has killed. She spits in his face. Only – typical of the Highsmith world – 'she missed his face, missed him entirely'.

Then Miss Highsmith goes on to write, almost the very last words of the book. 'Simone was just a trifle ashamed of herself, Tom thought. In that, she joined much of the rest of the world.' She joins us, we who need to learn the lesson that Patricia Highsmith teaches still. That we live in a dangerous, chancy world and the way to deal with it is, to quote Tom's specific advice to the boy in *The Boy Who*

Followed Ripley, to 'turn lose of' expectation and duties that are imposed not from necessity but from high-motived hypocrisy.

I once heard Miss Highsmith at a symposium on crime fiction in London recite with approval those lines of Browning that go, 'Our interest's on the dangerous edge of things. The honest thief, the tender murderer, the superstitious aetheist.' Tom, certainly, is that tender murderer, a person whom we cannot help liking for all that we stand in his shoes while he commits that blackest crime, and again and again. But Miss Highsmith's interest is not so much on the dangerous edge but deep in the middle of the dangerous seas.

And, although I have said it is our world of today that she paints for us, it should not be forgotten that, in fact, the world was never very much different for all the outward show of stability it has sometimes worn, at the height of Victorian opulence or in that period of tennis and tea parties we call the years between the wars. There are great writers who, before Miss Highsmith, saw the world in much the same light as she sees it. There is Kierkegaard, whom Tom actually once quotes. There is Gide with his *acte gratuit* of murder. There is Sartre.

But the Ripley books are crime stories. They bring us that world of doubt and darkness in a form designed first of all to entertain us. *The Talented Mr Ripley* is shot through with delightful deadpan humour. It is the final ingredient that makes the book, for all its picture of a rootless world, for all its murders committed by the man standing in our shoes, wonderfully readable, marvellously enjoyable.

A Taste for Death

In *A Taste for Death* P.D. James was able, at last, to give to the classical detective novel quality of scope. The book is a panorama. To a detective story in the classical form, with a mystery murder to be solved, with a gallery of suspects, with clues there for the seeing, Mrs James has added generous layers of life. What she did was to take each of the main figures of the case, suspects, discoverers of the bodies, the whole police team involved and show how the affair impinged on their lives, and to a very considerable depth.

She needed no fewer than 454 pages to do it in, as many as any major novel. But what she was doing, while still giving us a crime fiction, was to write, precisely, a novel on a major scale. All that length was necessary to show us in breadth and depth the whole effect of her murders on the people who came within their ambit.

With the full resources of the novelist she deals with the death by stabbing of Sir Paul Berowne, just resigned Minister of State in the British Government, together with that of an outcast tramp, Harry Mack, in the vestry of a church she imagined to exist – its architecture gives her an extra thrust, for all that it might seem an unnecessary addition – by the side of one of London's canals. To the lives affected by these killings she brings a compassionate judgement, an unassertive authority that is one of the gifts which the best women writers have for us.

She uses, as well, the full gamut of the resources of the English language – she is a notable public defender of the rich heritage of English – to describe the hunt for the perpetrator carried out by her detective of old, Commander Adam Dalgleish. It is a search for, as much as anything, the past of the chief and intended victim, Sir Paul, for what can be discovered 'through his dead body, through the intimate detritus of his life, through the mouths, truthful, treacherous, faltering, reluctant of his family, his enemies, his friends'. And these witnesses range from the boy of ten who is one of the discoverers of the body – that discovery, Mrs James believes, is a key point in the classical detective story – to Sir Paul's 82-year-old mother, a formidable lady indeed, from the top of the social scale to down near its foot.

But beyond this expansion of the detective story of old to new heights, depths and breadth, Mrs James has done something more in the book. She has been able, in it, to express her own profound beliefs on a subject of major concern. If earlier in *The Black Tower* she was able to write about real death in the context of the plaything deaths of the detective story, here she has been able to go further. She has written, in what might seem to be this unlikeliest of literary forms, a novel on the subject of faith, of faith in a life after death.

I do not think that hitherto there has been any crime fiction to which the background theme is religious belief. Of course, there have been a good many crime stories with priest, or vicar or rabbi as

P.D. James.

sleuth, and G.K. Chesterton's tales of Father Brown never hesitated to use aspects of the teaching of the Roman Catholic Church as Chesterton saw them to point the moral and adorn the tale. But that is what they were, adornments. Mrs James has made religious faith, whether we have it, how we can lose it, even how we can lose it and still have it, the very core of her book.

At first reading, one is unlikely to see this, and that, I believe is as it should be. The mystery story can work at a deep level, as deep as all

158

but the greatest novels. But it does so by stealth. Where with a serious novel the reader is ever alert for what it is going to tell him, with a detective novel that aims at any depth the reader ought to be simply engrossed in its story, in finding the answer to the ever-intriguing question 'Who did it?' But, underneath, what the writer has put into the book, whether consciously or even unconsciously, will be having its effect. And, I venture to claim, that effect will be all the more telling for being put over in that secret manner.

But re-read *A Taste for Death* with a mind alert and the evidence, not as to who done it, but as to what Mrs James has done will be clear. Consider the setting of the murders: a church. Consider, when it emerges, the fact that Sir Paul first visited the church out of a casual interest in architecture but there was struck by a revelation, no less. Consider where the clinching clue comes to light: in that same church revisited. Look at the final pages, where one might expect a summing-up: what do we get? Not the revelation of the murderer's name, that has come well before, at about page 364. Instead we get a last glimpse of the elderly lady who, with the boy, discovered the body, and what is she doing? Praying for faith.

Or consider what Sir Paul's mother, the sharp-tongued Lady Ursula, says to Commander Dalgleish as he attempts to secure glimpses of her son's life from her. She evades his questioning. But how? By telling him she has had a visit from the priest in whose church her son died. 'He seemed to me,' she says,

> a man who has long ago given up the expectation of influencing anyone. Perhaps he has lost his faith. Isn't that fashionable in the Church today? But why should that distress him? The world is full of people who have lost faith; politicians who have lost faith in politics, social workers who have lost faith in social work, school-teachers who have lost faith in teaching and, for all I know, policemen who have lost faith in policing and poets who have lost faith in poetry.

These last two examples, sharp digs at Dalgleish, whom we see as, if not having lost all faith in his two careers as investigator and as maker of poems, at least as filled with doubts on both scores.

So, all through a book that has for most of its length that old, safe tug of who-done-it and which has, after that has been surrendered, a passage of strong and highly suspenseful action, the workings of this major theme. No wonder I rate it among the very highest, and most readable, achievements of the crime writer's art.

4 GOOD OLD BOYS

R. Austin Freeman

Just recently I was a little startled to see reproduced a photograph of myself, loomingly black-bearded, standing beside a white-bearded Mr Michael Heenan, flanked by the Mayor and Mayoress of Gravesend, Kent, wearing their chains of office, with in front of us a simple tombstone bearing the words *Richard Austin Freeman 1862-1943 Physician and Author Erected by the Friends of 'Dr Thorndyke'*. I realised then that some nine years had passed and my own sable beard had silvered since the day we had gathered to unveil that long-overdue memorial.

Besides Mr Heenan, industrious commentator on Dr Thorndyke's cases, there was present then, though modestly avoiding the camera, my fellow crime writer Catherine Aird, as well as generous American contributors to the cost of the stone. I remember now I had been asked to say a few words. But what words they were I can by no means recall. What I ought to have said, and perhaps did, was that the books about Dr Thorndyke had given me enormous pleasure when I had read them as a boy, that I counted myself in however small a way Austin Freeman's heir, and that those books, if a little dated, are good value still.

One in particular I remember well from a later than boyhood reading, not really because of its seemingly odd title, *The Mystery of Angelina Frood*, but because that title indicates what the book is, an ingenious attempt to 'finish' Dickens's marvellous unfinished *The Mystery of Edwin Drood*, in a contemporary setting and in the countryside that Dr Freeman knew well, the area round Gravesend where he lived long and now lies buried.

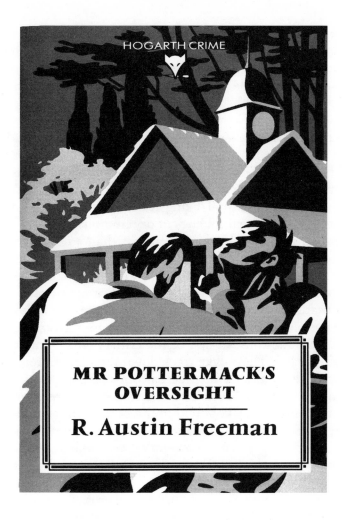

Who was Dr Thorndyke whose name shares that gravestone? What manner of man? Dr Freeman himself answered the question in a broadcast talk given when his detective stories were at the height of their fame. To discover his origin, he said then, he had to reach back at least 50 years to when he was a medical student himself and gave particular attention to 'the legal aspects of medicine and the medical aspects of law'. The classic cases, of poisoning, of identification, had fascinated him. But he had had his way to make as a doctor and 'all this curious lore was put away for the time being in the pigeon-holes of my mind – which Dr Freud would call the Unconscious'.

Then, when failing health forced him to give up the arduous practice of medicine, the notion of writing fiction with this background re-surfaced. He went on to say that Thorndyke himself had come to life when, working at Westminster Ophthalmic Hospital, it had struck him that a complex prescription for spectacles might well be an almost infallible clue to identity. He wrote a book, *The Red Thumb-mark*, with a medico-legal expert in it to make the recognition. He called his man Thorndyke.

And, because he believed 'a first-class man of any kind usually tends to be a good-looking man' (Reader, peer into the mirror), he made Thorndyke 'handsome and of an imposing presence, with a symmetrical face of the classical type and a Grecian nose'. He has, a concession, 'an unnatural liking for Trichinopoly cheroots', and is 'addicted to occasional touches of dry humour'.

He was an investigator of crime rather than a detective, and the readers of his cases might be expected to know a few curious scientific facts, though in the end Thorndyke always explains them, at full length, to his friend Jervis. It is in the application of such facts to a mystery that Dr Thorndyke worked, and there are even short stories, and one particularly good novel, *Mr Pottermack's Oversight*, that are 'inverted', that is, we read first of the crime being committed, then pleasurably watch Thorndyke track down the perpetrator.

This may seem a fairly intellectual pursuit, and Austin Freeman knew that it was. He believed detective stories could reach respectable heights, but only if they kept within the bounds they should possess. In a long article in a magazine *The Nineteenth Century* (which ran on after the year 1901 as *The Nineteenth Century and After* but never embarrassingly reached 2001) he castigated the books often crassly confounded with detective stories, the mere thrillers, saying that the ever-escalating dilemma of 'the purveyor of gross sensationalism' was in effect that of the sportsman in 'the juvenile verse'

I shoot the hippopotamus with bullets made of platinum
Because if I use leaden ones his hide is bound to flatten 'em.

The real connoisseurs, he goes on, 'are to be found among men of the definitely intellectual class: theologians, scholars, lawyers, and to a less extent, perhaps, doctors and men of science. Judging by the letters which I have received from time to time, the enthusiast *par excellence* is the clergyman of studious and scholarly habit.' But I think us lesser mortals, even women, can still read the books with enjoyment. Soberish enjoyment perhaps, but enjoyment, even if we fall short of the full intellectual rigour.

162

Melville Davisson Post

Melville Davisson Post was a lawyer born in West Virginia in 1869. Towards the end of his life he ran the Democratic national presidential campaign in 1924. His candidate lost: Calvin Coolidge won. He was a successful commercial short-story writer and the creator of the wicked lawyer, Randolph Mason. To this he added such cosmopolitan characters as Monsieur Jonquelle, prefect of the Paris Police, Sir Henry Marquis, 'the sleuth of St James's Square' and Walker of the Secret Service. But it is for his tales of Uncle Abner, Virginia law-enforcer of the days when the backlands knew no policing, that he deserves never to be forgotten.

Yet, sadly, he has hardly had a chance to be much remembered on Sir Henry Marquis's side of the Atlantic. An occasional Uncle Abner story has appeared in anthologies. But, although in America the tales, originally all written for magazines, were collected in book form as long ago as 1918, it was not until 1972 that *Uncle Abner, Master of Mysteries* appeared in Britain, and it is now out of print. Quite why Uncle Abner has not become as widely known in Britain as Chesterton's Father Brown, whose exploits (if that is the word) appeared originally at much the same time as Abner's, is hard to say.

It can hardly be because Melville Davisson Post did not tell a gripping story. By making the description of the mystery and the development towards its solution go on side by side, he once said, the formula 'very markedly increases the rapidity of the action . . . holds the reader's attention throughout, and eliminates any impression of moving at any time over ground previously covered'. And what he preached he practised.

But, more, he not only told a swift story but he was also capable of producing solutions to his mysteries that rival those of Conan Doyle. And in Uncle Abner he created a fine, original, believable character. He has him bring to his self-imposed task of uncovering crime two sterling attributes: keen observation and a deep knowledge of and love for the Bible.

His keenness of observation can be seen in the story 'An Act of God' when, at the end, Abner explains that a man who was deaf could not have written a letter which has a word in it mis-spelt

D. Millsap's illustration showing Uncle Abner viewing the body.

phonetically. And the first Abner story, 'The Doomdorf Mystery', is a locked-room tale to rival the best.

It is in this, too, that we can see Abner's love of the Bible, and what it gives to him in moral strength. When the 'Watson', the somewhat pompous yet brave Squire Randolph, asks under what statute of the law of Virginia the crime should be punished, Abner replies grimly that the punishment should come 'under an authority somewhat higher', the Biblical injunction 'He that killeth with the sword must be killed by the sword.' He goes on: 'Must! Randolph, did you mark particularly the word *must*? It is a mandatory law. There is no room in it for the vicissitudes of chance or fortune. There is no way round that word. Thus we reap what we sow.' There's moral grandeur for you. And in the solution of the mystery that stern law simply operates.

But if Abner is tough he is also patently good (and how comforting it is to have toughness on the Good's side). Asked, in the story 'Naboth's Vineyard', what can be the motive for the crime, Abner replies it is to be found 'in the twenty-first chapter of the Book of Kings'. The reader, however lacking in detailed knowledge of the Bible, has been alerted, to some extent, by the story's title: Naboth's vineyard was coveted by one prepared to use any means to acquire it. And ruthless acquisitiveness is the key to why a man is standing trial for his life in a Virginian court-room, and why Uncle Abner rises up, startling as Perry Mason, and turns the case upside down.

Edgar Wallace

If one set out to find the most colourful crime writer in all the years, Edgar Wallace would surely rank high. His whole life was colourful in the extreme, and heartening. Born in 1875, the son of an actor and actress, out of wedlock, he was adopted almost at once by a Billingsgate fish porter, to whom in his autobiography he paid warm tribute. Here he is: 'Said yer prayers?' 'Yes, father.' Pause. 'You'll go to hell if yer don't.' 'Yes, father.' Longer pause. 'I don't know that yer will.'

Even as a boy Edgar Wallace showed vividly the talents that were to make him, in his own words, 'one atom that climbed out of the thick mud'. Asked one day by a stranger to take a coin to a tobacconist and get change, he promptly sought out a policeman, showed him what he had been given and asked 'Is this snide?' A forgery it was, and, despite all temptation, our hero had chosen the side of the good. Or at least the fairly good. Soon he was to be found 'hopping the wag' from school to sell newspapers at a particularly windy corner of Fleet Street – a plaque now marks the spot. But what was he doing to keep himself warm? Rampageously reciting Shakespeare.

In and out of jobs thereafter he ended up in the Army and was sent out to South Africa. There he offered precocious and fairly awful verses to visiting Rudyard Kipling, bought himself out of military service and set up as a newspaperman, contriving when peace negotiations were being conducted behind a barbed-wire fence a simple system of signalling with coloured handkerchiefs that gave him a world scoop.

Back in England, he continued as a journalist, evidently with a nose for a story. When during the Russo-Japanese War the Russian fleet was sailing in fog through the North Sea and fired on some English fishing-boats, Wallace was sent to its first port of call, Vigo, in Spain, and learnt from two petty officers that their commander had actually believed he was being attacked by a Japanese force. The *Daily Mail* found this hard to credit – Who wouldn't? – and sent Wallace to the fleet's next port, Tangier, to get confirmation. And what did he find there? His two informants had been executed and buried at sea.

So perhaps one can hardly blame him for the element of the extraordinary that marked his writing when he turned from journalism to crime fiction. In 1905 he published at his own expense *The Four Just Men*, keeping back the solution of its mystery and offering a money prize to anyone who guessed it. The book sold tremendously: too many readers out-guessed its author: result, misery. But Wallace wrote on, prolifically and at high speed. His final tally amounted to 173 books, one of them *The Coat of Arms* written non-stop over one weekend, and not bad at that.

Others have startling flaws, such as characters changing their names half-way through and miraculous escapes on the lines of 'With one bound, Jack . . .', and action that is, to say the least, unlikely as in *The Three Oaks Mystery* where a grieviously wounded character not only scales a 14-foot wall topped with broken glass but also proves to be the heroine's father.

But there are compensating virtues. Wallace told a cracking story. 'I write to amuse,' he said once. And that he did, to the extent of being an enormous bestseller. His crime heroes, too, if fairly two-dimensional, are easy to stand in the shoes of – prim Mr J.G. Reeder in whose office 'the turning of a paper produced a gentle disturbance' and yet who is a deadly shot, even Derrick Yale, 'the amazing psychometrical detective', and the melancholy Elk of *The Fellowship of the Frog*.

So from the lowliest of beginnings by the sheer fecundity of his imagination Wallace made a huge fortune, and splurged it, on suites

at London hotels, on a yellow Rolls-Royce, on marvellously unsuccessful racecourse betting, coupled with acting as a tipster in the press. No wonder his children called him 'Krazy', after the cartoon cat. And how warmly typical that he let them.

His end was in keeping with the image of himself he put abroad, the magnificently careless and luckily successful, an image that his books, and the plays that were as much of a public draw, reflected. He was invited to Hollywood. He contributed to the script of *King Kong*. He fell ill from overwork and, in 1932, he died. His body was brought back to England, and a tumultuous reception, by Blue Riband liner. He left enormous debts. Within a few years sales of his books wiped them out. And the books are still re-issued and re-read.

Jacques Futrelle

Jacques Futrelle, a journalist who was born in Pike County, Georgia, in 1875 and died when the *Titanic* sank in 1912, wrote one of the finest crime short stories ever to be committed to paper. Called 'The Problem of Cell 13', it first appeared as a serial in a Boston paper in 1905 and featured Futrelle's creation, Professor S.F.X. Van Dusen, known as The Thinking Machine. In the course of his short life Futrelle also produced stories about The Thinking Machine almost as breathtakingly ingenious as his masterpiece, and others less good, in a total of some 50, as well as a handful of novels with mystery elements and, towards his last days, frothy romances.

What he would have done as a writer if on that terrible night of 15 April 1912, he had not pushed his wife into one of the *Titanic's* lifeboats but refused to get in himself must be a matter of speculation. He might never have written in the crime field again; he might have produced work to put even 'The Problem of Cell 13' in the shade. It is not unknown for authors to have little idea of what they are really doing.

Even in that masterpiece story we cannot be sure that Futrelle consciously knew just what it is about it that makes it so grippingly memorable. Outwardly it is no more than a piece of tremendous ingenuity, written in an agreeably light manner. It concerns a bet made by the professor in a moment of petulance that, if locked up in the death-cell in Chisholm Prison under the customary rigorous conditions, he could get out by the sheer power of thought within a week.

The story merely details the ingenious series of things Van Dusen does to get himself out of that cell. The use of a rat to take a message out through a disused drainpipe is one of them, as is Van Dusen's reliance on the ordinary person's distaste for a dead rat as the means by which he conceals his discovery of the drainpipe as his tenuous link with the outside world.

But what is not often noted is the fact that Futrelle did not actually get his prisoner out of Cell 13 purely by implacable logic. He had the professor rely, too, quite largely, on the sort of intuitive thinking that can also be called common sense.

The notion of the repulsiveness of a dead rat is one example. Although the story purports to be a proof of the professor's axiom that 'the mind is the master of all things', in fact he succeeds in his 'impossible' task through a mixture of logic and simple imagination.

Elsewhere, in the story 'Kidnapped Baby Blake, Millionaire', Futrelle has The Thinking Machine say indeed, 'Imagination is necessary to supply temporary gaps caused by absence of facts. Imagination is the backbone of the scientific mind. Marconi had to imagine wireless telegraphy before he accomplished it.' This is that combination of two, apparently opposed, powers of the mind which Edgar Allan Poe saw as necessary for the creation of that myth hero, the Great Detective, the rational and the intuitive. It puts Futrelle's protagonist squarely among such figures.

Yet in view of Futrelle's quite ordinary career as a journalist and the fairly humdrum novels and stories he was capable of writing, one is entitled to ask: did he at all know what he was doing? Had he in 'The Problem of Cell 13' deceived not only his many readers but also himself? Did he consciously set out to include in this story apparently of the implacable workings of a super-mind those elements of simple, intuitive common sense which in fact give it that extra which has made it so appealing over the years?

Well, to borrow a nice phrase from a study of Futrelle's story by Professor Benedict Freeman: a writer is not obliged to have good diplomatic relations with his unconscious. Sometimes, we know, the unconscious simply invades the conscious mind to produce ideas that the daylight brain could never have envisaged. So probably Futrelle just wrote – and produced, possibly never knowing what he had done before his premature death, an enduring work of art.

Professor S.F.X. Van Dusen behind the bars of Cell 13.

3 GOOD OLD GIRLS

Mary Roberts Rinehart

Mary Roberts Rinehart, declares Dorothy B. Hughes, crime critic and novelist, 'has been and continues to be' the most important American woman mystery writer. And, since the Rinehart mystery novels were written between 1908 and 1952, this is a considerable claim to make. However, it is easy to justify, despite what might be seen as the author's easy-come huge commercial success, as well as because of that.

Born in Pittsburgh in 1876, daughter of an unsuccessful and impecunious inventor, Mary Roberts trained as a nurse, but three days after graduating at the age of 19 she married Dr Stanley Rinehart and in the ensuing five years gave him three sons (two became publishers, the third a writer). After the crash of 1903, however, the young Rineharts found themselves in debt. So Mary set to and wrote short stories, 45 within a year, all sold to a leading magazine.

Its editors then suggested she write them a serial. This was the very successful *The Man in Lower Ten*, rapidly followed by *The Circular Staircase*, which, published in book form first, was to become her most famous work, later, as *The Bat*, made into a play and a film and re-novelised by its author and one Avery Hopwood in 1926.

At one time Mary Roberts Rinehart was America's highest paid author. Altogether she wrote some 20 mystery novels, many short stories and 16 romantic novels. She added two to the tally of high-profile sleuths. There is Miss Letitia Carberry, known as 'Tish',

perhaps only a marginal detective and more a figure designed to get into farcical situations. And there is Nurse Hilda Adams, otherwise 'Miss Pinkerton', a lady who, called in to look after any invalid, was apt to send the threat of murder swooshing along in front of her like the ominous wave that heralds a hurricane, but who, mercifully, seemed able to desert beds of sickness at frequent enough intervals to unmask the killers.

The Rinehart career was crowned with a Mystery Writers of America Special Award a year after she published her last novel, *The Swimming Pool*, and by the award, as early as 1923, of an honorary Doctorate in Literature from George Washington University.

One might think the latter excessive for a purely popular writer. But such is not the case. Certainly, Mary Roberts Rinehart knew how to make her books gulpingly readable. She saw to it always that the reader was able completely to identify emotionally with the heroines she wrote about. (The books are more popular with women readers, but a man, unless he be very concerned about his macho status, can easily tag along.) And she adroitly set against considerable violence a strong and evident strain of romance. In her 1938 book, *The Wall*, she said once, 'I commit three shocking murders in a New England summer colony.' But she committed one beautiful romance as well.

For this and for similar books (*The Album* of 1933, of which she said 'The answer to four gruesome murders lies in a dusty album') she perhaps did not merit her high academic honour. But for what she did in *The Circular Staircase* she undoubtedly did.

Outwardly the book is the simple story of a spinster lady, Rachel Innes, who takes a summer house with her niece and nephew and finds herself involved in a series of mysterious happenings culminating in her being trapped in a black, windowless secret room with a murderer ('There was someone else in the darkness, someone who breathed hard and was so close I could have touched him by the hand') and eventually triumphs. But, whether consciously or not, Mary Roberts Rinehart produced underneath this gothic flim-flam a profound symbolic unfolding.

Despite being told in a manner which Ogden Nash was later to stigmatise as the 'Had I But Known' style (See 'The Oxblood Book of Detectival Verse'), a method largely dictated by the needs of the original serial publication, *The Circular Staircase* is, to quote its very first words, 'the story of how a middle-aged spinster lost her mind', sank, that is, the purely rational in the intuitive. For 20 years, Rachel

Innes says, she had been 'perfectly comfortable' but then 'the madness seized me'.

So what we read of underneath is a battle between the rational and the irrational, between Miss Rachel's common sense and the 'ghosts' that are spoken of as haunting the old house. It is a battle, too, between daylight and the dark, splendidly evoked in the image of the electric company switching off the power at midnight each day with the lights 'fading slowly until there is only a red-hot loop to be seen in the bulb'.

All the characters in the book divide into day and dark people. The men are daylight fellows, realistic and down-to-earth. The women, with the exception of Miss Rachel, are fluttery, irrational and all too ready to believe in the spectres of the night. So it is Miss Rachel who, like the Great Detective created by Edgar Allan Poe 'both creative . . . and resolvent', combines at last the intuitive and the rational, climbs the circular staircase that is a feature of the old house (but which serves no particular outward purpose in the story) and winds her way to the heart of the mystery.

In doing so she puts in front of us, ready completely for our emotional involvement, a story which 80 years after it was written still has power to hold us. A secret power.

Gladys Mitchell

Great Detectives, Professor George Grella, one of the best and subtlest critics of mystery fiction, has said, can be divided into three kinds. Most of those in the classic Golden Age days were the Gentleman Amateur. But there was also the Elf (Hercule Poirot is one, Father Brown another) and there was the Wizard, such as Rex Stout's infallible Nero Wolfe or John Dickson Carr's equally magisterial Dr Fell. To these last, changing perhaps wizard to witch, can be added Gladys Mitchell's Dame Beatrice Adela Lestrange Bradley.

Dame Beatrice, or plain Mrs Bradley as she was in 1929 when she came to life in Gladys Mitchell's first crime story, *Speedy Death*, was not in fact destined then to be the sleuth. 'I'd got this man called Carstairs,' Miss Mitchell said in an interview when her 50th book, the delightfully nostalgic *Late, Late in the Evening* came out in 1976. 'Mrs Bradley was just one of the house guests. But she sort of took over.' She did, indeed, appearing in all 66 of the Mitchell mysteries.

You can see why. To begin with, she had the useful profession for an amateur detective of psychiatrist (think of Helen McCloy's, Dr Basil Willing), and she was attached (vaguely) to the Home Office which is in charge (vaguely) of Britain's police. But, more important, Dame Beatrice is a wonderfully flamboyant lady. In looks she has been described as lizard-like, crocodile-like, as having a yellow face and a smile like a boa constrictor's with hands like claws. And she dressed generally in a way that can only be called garish. Magenta was a favourite colour. And when she laughed she cackled.

Yet she had a beautiful voice and in youth 'had been followed by strange men'. In those days, however, her creator said, she had been 'a black-haired, brilliant-eyed siren, ugly, vivacious, unfashionably thin and small, but possessing an attractiveness which, though entirely divorced from physical beauty, exercised a kind of electric current upon those who came in contact with her. It accounted for her popularity with both sexes and with all age-groups and it probably accounted (in both senses) for the three husbands who had predeceased her.'

A touch in those last words there, from *Lament for Leto*, of the sharp unorthodoxy that enlivens the Mitchell books, such as her bland statement in *When Last I Died* that Mrs Bradley advocated euthanasia for totally incorrigible young delinquents. The quality is to be seen, too, in the murder Mrs Bradley commits herself in her detectival debut, and, once found Not Guilty, happily admits to, as well as on the occasions when like Sherlock Holmes before her she decides a murderer ought to go free. 'It's always interesting to behave abominably,' she cheerfully says in *My Bones Will Keep*.

Again, this unorthodoxy is to be seen in Mrs Bradley's delight in one of her ancestors having been a witch. And this, indeed, is what she herself is, though a white witch rather than a black. She exists to make all well, which, as Professor Grella has pointed out, is the function of certain characters in comedy and has been so throughout the ages.

Gladys Mitchell well realised, in fact, that her books had about them the basic unreality of all-ends-well comedy (an unreality which may yet be a higher reality). 'I regard my books as fairy tales,' she said. 'I never take the crime itself seriously.' And she says of Dame Beatrice, 'She has this soft spot for young people. I can't help that because it's in me.' But in fiction, as not alas in real life, the young can be brought to happy endings, as they are in all the best classical comedies. The wizard, or witch, works the magic. Good old Prospero.

Perhaps some of this decisive, judge-like attitude came from Dame Beatrice's creator's long years as a school teacher. She taught, altogether for some 37 years at a variety of ordinary state schools, English, history and games. Even at one stage, having been brought up in full equality with her brothers, passing on her skills as a boxer to a generation of small boys far beneath her, recalling with laughter the time when one of them, invited to try to dot her on the nose, succeeded all too bloodily. Her ability to think as a small boy herself is well shown in *The Rising of the Moon*, her own favourite of all her books, partly told in the voice of a 13-year-old.

So year by year Gladys Mitchell gave the world a new case for Mrs Bradley, or latterly Dame Beatrice. The books varied widely in subject, however (and sometimes, it should be acknowledged in quality). As the poet Philip Larkin said of her, she always 'stood splendidly apart from her crime-club confrères in total originality . . . blending eccentricity of subject matter with authoritative common-sense of style.'

Mrs Bradley was not the first female detective. Others had come long before her, mostly in magazine stories. But they were short-lived, and, worse, they were required to be of a femininity altogether too much (Anna Katherine Green's Violet Stranger of 1915 was 'vivacity incarnate . . . light as thistledown in fibre and in feeling'). But Mrs Bradley pipped Agatha Christie's Miss Marple to the post at least in book form, though Ms Christie's short stories about her pussy-cat detective were already about, and she came close on the heels of Patricia Wentworth's Marple seem-alike Miss Maud Silver. What was it, one wonders, about the late 1920s that made elderly detectives spring up?

In 1979 Gladys Mitchell had said to an interviewer, with charac-teristic forthrightness, that her publishers were pressing her for more books. 'I think they feel I'm likely to die on them at any moment.' It was not until 1983, however, that her long life came to an end, and that was not without leaving two titles to be published posthumously.

Margery Allingham

Agatha Christie, paying tribute to Margery Allingham shortly after her death in 1966, said that, instead of asking whether she herself read others' detective stories, people ought to ask her how many of those she did read (since 'having the same bright idea concerning a murder will result in an indignant complaint from readers') she was able to remember. 'Not very many,' she answers, with that lemon-zest sharpness she sometimes had. But, she added, 'Margery Allingham stands out like a shining light.'

Margery Allingham was not quite so nice about Agatha Christie when I interviewed her many years ago for a magazine called, I think, *Town*, then owned by a young and ambitious Michael Heseltine, subsequently Mrs Margaret Thatcher's Minister of Defence. 'People are always lumping me in with Agatha Christie,' she said then. 'But I could give her 15 years.'

She could indeed. Her first book came out when she was 18, in 1921, while Mrs Christie, though *The Mysterious Affair of Styles* beat by one year *Blackerchief Dick*, a tale of piracy paranormally dictated to the adolescent Margery on the ouija board (or, if you prefer, by her subconscious), was at that time almost 30.

But Margery Allingham was brought up to write, and lived all her life to write, saying charmingly of herself in middle age that she had a figure designed for great endurance at a desk. 'My father wrote,' she said. 'My mother wrote, all the weekend visitors wrote and, as soon as I could master the appallingly difficult business of making the initial marks, so did I.' Before quitting school, at 15, she had written a play and acted in it. Then she produced fiction for the *Sexton Blake* juvenile crime magazine and hammered out 'the story of the film' for something called *Girls Cinema*. In 1928 she produced a serial for the *Daily Express* called *The Crime at Black Dudley* and that brought to the world Mr Albert Campion.

At that stage Mr Campion was something of a caricature. He had a falsetto voice and his teeth protruded, though underneath like Baroness Orczy's Scarlet Pimpernel he was terribly brave. When in the following year *Mystery Mile* appeared he is a little more outwardly with it, perhaps because in that book he is seen to have

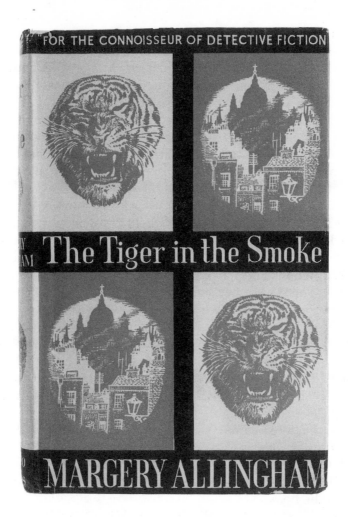

as his 'man' the elephantinely commonsensical and lugubrious Magersfontein Lugg. With *Police at the Funeral* in 1931 Mr Campion tackled more serious matters, and so book by book, with sometimes a pause, sometimes even a slight recession, he becomes more and more responsible.

As, indeed, he should have been, if we are to believe what his creator once said of him to the distinguished novelist, Pamela Hansford Johnson. In her autobiographical book, *Important to Me*, published in 1974, she says that meeting Margery Allingham at a party and finding her 'surpassingly amiable' she asked what eventually became of Mr Campion, whose high social status beneath that *nom de guerre* is often hinted at in the early books. 'Oh,' Margery

Allingham is reported as saying simply, 'he came to the Throne.' So was he or was he not His Majesty King George VI, who unexpectedly came to the Throne when his elder brother abdicated?

Whatever the truth, or party put-down, of that, we see Mr Campion at work after World War II (while George VI inhabited Buckingham Palace). And it is a yet more changed Campion we see. For the long last part of the war Margery Allingham left him in abeyance while she buckled to with war work herself and produced, at the instigation of her American publisher, a factual book about rural Britain under fire, *The Oaken Heart*.

'He had changed a little,' she wrote of Campion in 1945 in *Coroner's Pigeon*, which begins with him just returned from unspecified work as an agent, lying in his first bath at his home in the flat in 'Bottle Street', Piccadilly, 'the sun had bleached his fair hair to whiteness, lending him a physical distinction he had never before possessed. There were new lines in his over-thin face and with their appearance some of his own misleading vacancy of expression had vanished.' In other words, the Wodehousian idiot of 1929 – the figure who had made young Agatha Christie wonder whether the Margery Allingham she had never met might be Dorothy Sayers, (whose Lord Peter then was fairly Woosterish), under a pseudonym – was to be the magisterial observer of human follies of 1945 and on.

And so the books came, in ever increasing sureness. In 1948, *More Work for the Undertaker* was published – that splendidly rich novel, replete with portraits of wonderful eccentrics, among them the Scotland Yarder, Charlie Luke. Listen to him describing the old doctor in the book:

> Comes out of his flat nagged to a rag in the mornings and goes down into his surgery-room with a shopfront like a laundry. Seven-and-six for a visit, half a dollar for a squint at your tonsils or a thorough once-over if he isn't sure, and a bottle of muck which does you good. Stooping. Back like a camel . . .

It's a magnificently energetic portrait, both of the doctor and of Luke.

Then in 1952 there was *The Tiger in the Smoke*, that battle between Good and Evil at full stretch, praised to the skies by many, though earning a sharp rebuke from Graham Greene.

And finally *The Mind Readers* in 1965 and, last of all, *A Cargo of Eagles*, uncompleted at her death in 1966 but put together, a shadow of what might have been, by her husband, the illustrator Philip Youngman-Carter.

2 INTO ONE

Ellery Queen
Fred Dannay and Manfred Lee

The story has often been told. In New York in 1928 *McClure's Magazine* and the publishing house of Stokes announced a competition for a detective story with a hefty prize. Two cousins, Fred Dannay and Manfred Lee, decided to enter, wrote a book called *The Roman Hat Mystery*, extraordinarily ingenious, and were let know before the official announcement that their attempt, written, since entries had to be pseudonymous, as Ellery Queen, had won.

Then *McClure's* folded. The magazine *Smart Set* took over, decided another entry, by a lady called Isabel Briggs Myers, would better please women readers and gave the prize to that. Stokes, however, decided to publish Ellery Queen's *The Roman Hat Mystery*, featuring their detective, also called Ellery Queen – James Griffen and Wilbur See rejected as names – and the two cousins went on to collaborate on book after book over the years, with such success that both became nicely wealthy men. Isabel Briggs Myers wrote one other crime story and then faded into oblivion.

The history raises, of course, an intriguing question. Somehow we think of works of fiction as being the products of one unique mind. How, then, can two people produce such a work? Generally, they cannot. The exceptions often are when a person with some skill with words fleshes out an idea that has come to one of nature's non-writers, quite frequently someone with a name, acquired, say, on the sports field. But there are occasions when two human beings seem to see things so much in the same way that collaboration produces fiction better than either might have risen to alone.

Such clearly was the case with Fred Dannay and Manfred Lee,

WHOMEVER

If I erred in originally choosing *The Player on the Other Side* by 'Ellery Queen' for my *Crime and Mystery: the 100 Best Books* only to have it set aside on learning it was in all probability the work of another writer than Queen, I erred in good company. William DeAndrea, author of comic crime novels featuring Matt Cobb, TV company detective, and others as well as winner of Mystery Writers of America awards (alas, not published in Britain, yet) selecting his ten favourite mystery novels for the magazine *Armchair Detective*, picked *The Player on the Other Side* as one of them.

Here's what he had to say about it: 'This book changed my life . . . and made a raving mystery fan (and therefore ultimately a mystery writer) out of me.' If you believed, he went on, that the murderer in Agatha Christie's *Roger Ackroyd* was a surprise, 'God knows this one will be a shock.' If, he added, the rumour is correct that Theodore Sturgeon, the science-fiction author, actually wrote it from an outline by the other-half of 'Ellery Queen', Fred Dannay, the book must be 'one of the most skilful pastiches in the history of literature'.

It has, William DeAndrea says (and I concur), the oblique approaches, the slightly-too-clever dialogue, the religious themes, the constant weaving of the clues in the very language that mark it out as the apotheosis of the Queen novel. 'An amazing piece of work, whomever did it.'

though they went to great pains never to say just how they worked as one. But they were, to begin with, first cousins. There were born, too, in the same year, 1905. They had much the same upbringing, Jewish life and customs in crowded, street-tough Brooklyn, to the point of their mothers having the same physician at the births, a dominating figure who marched off and registered the two babes, Daniel Nathan and Emanuel Lepofsky, himself. Both quite early in life changed their names to the forms we know them by today.

So they had a great deal in common, including a dislike of

violence, heritage of the days when both had sought refuge from the fracas of the streets in head-buried reading. But they also differed. In temperament the two close cousins were by no means alike. Fred Dannay was quiet and scholarly (he was eventually to amass and comment learnedly upon the greatest collection yet brought together of crime short stories), an introvert and a perfectionist. Manfred Lee, who looked very much like his cousin, short in stature, spectacle-wearing, eventually bearded, was an extrovert, impulsive, explosive, free with the cuss-words. They believed they said, in what little they let out about their collaboration, that the clash of temperament gave their writing a sharper edge. Fred Dannay once admitted, 'We're not so much collaborators as competitors.'

But how actually did they do it? Did they sit together and hammer the stuff out word by word? Did one write the dialogue and the other the narration? Certainly, at one time, in the early 1930s they were known each to work, for up to 12 hours a day, in their own homes and to meet just once a week in a small bare office in a building at Columbus Circle. But apparently what eventually happened was that Fred Dannay, in principle, produced the plots, the clues and what would have to be deduced from them as well as the outlines of the characters and Manfred Lee clothed it all in

Fred Dannay (left) and Manfred Lee.

words. But it is unlikely to have been as clear cut as that.

The two, who also collaborated in their early days as 'Barnaby Ross' with a retired Shakespearian actor, Drury Lane, as sleuth, were very much one. At one time they went about performing a sort of double act. Fred Dannay would, behind a mask, announce himself as Barnaby Ross, and Manfred Lee, equally masked, would state he was Ellery Queen. People said Ross must be the wit and critic Alexander Woolcott and Queen S.S. Van Dine (real name Huntington Willard Wright), creator of the super-snob detective Philo Vance, on whom 'Ellery Queen' was indeed modelled. Later the cousins took a sharper view of Vance, Manfred Lee calling him, with typical vehemence, 'the biggest prig that ever came down the pike'.

After some six books the cousins began to throw off the Van Dine influence and to change Ellery Queen, detective, into a much more human, sympathetic character, one to whom Dashiell Hammett's well-known public enquiry, 'Mr Queen, will you be good enough to explain your famous character's sex life, if any?' less and less applied.

In the books towards the end – Manfred Lee died in 1971 and no further titles appeared – the matter of collaboration, however, is yet further complicated. If rumour and digging-out mean anything, other writers were eventually allowed to share in the pie.

It was a complication that fearsomely caught me out myself. I had almost finished writing my *Crime and Mystery: the 100 Best Books*, in which I had included both Ellery Queen's *Calamity Town* and the later *The Player on the Other Side*. My piece on the latter, though I say it, was a fine example of thoughtful literary criticism, placing the book squarely in the Queen canon. Then Geoff Bradley, editor of *Cads*, the magazine about crime-writing, sent me an article stating explicitly that the book had been written entirely by a third author, the science-fiction writer Theodore Sturgeon. So much for the unique identity of the two cousins who united themselves as Ellery Queen.

Emma Lathen
Jane Latsis and Martha Henissart

My copy of John C. Carr's book of interviews with mystery writers, *The Craft of Crime*, has a title page inscription 'A small reminder of a pleasant evening' signed 'Emma Lathen'. But which half, I ask, of Emma Lathen wielded that actual pen? I had seen for myself in the flesh the two witty and nice American ladies, Jane Latsis and Martha Henissart, who together produce the Emma Lathen books, a true symbiosis, 'the living together of two dissimilar organisms in more or less intimate association or close union', though, in fact, I had learnt that the two have separate apartments and meet together in the country only occasionally.

As a mystery writer, however, that dictionary definition of 'symbiosis' pretty well describes the 'author' of the long crime saga featuring John Putnam Thatcher, of the Wall Street banking firm Sloan Guaranty Trust (and his perfect, steel-plated secretary, Miss Corsa) and of the shorter saga, written as R.B. Dominic, featuring Congressman Ben Stafford amid the complexities and occasional criminalities of Washington DC. In a quite extraordinary way the two succeed in writing seamless prose. And, more extraordinary, they do it by writing alternate chapters.

Part of this success can be accounted by the intellectual similarity of its two contributors. Both Jane Latsis and Martha Henissart are Harvard graduates, the former holding a doctorate in agricultural economics and the latter a law degree. Both, too, worked for major institutions before they joined together as writers, or perhaps I should say as a writer. Jane Latsis was with the UN Food and Agriculture Organisation and Martha Henissart was in corporate finance and banking.

They both share, too, a vacuum-cleaner-like ability to absorb facts, but contrive to empty them much less messily. When in 1976 I asked the pair if they would contribute to a book of essays I was compiling, *Agatha Christie: First Lady of Crime* – but which one of them did I write to? – they succeeded in amassing a tremendous slew of facts about Agatha in America and also in presenting them with stiletto humour.

This is their method in their mystery stories, a kind of literature each read voraciously before they met at Harvard. Their books are packed with facts about whatever field of finance they have decided to thrust poor John Putnam Thatcher into. In their debut book, it is banking: in others the auto industry, real estate, even oriental rugs, grain sales to Soviet Russia and, hardest hitting of all, the American medical profession.

Then to the facts they add, in whichever chapter, prickles of teasing wit. The result, miraculously, is one delectable whole.

NOW READ ELSEWHERE

Once upon a time there was scarcely anything written about crime fiction in general. There were one or two rather ponderous histories, very much with eyes on the distant past, and there was a how-to-do-it or two. Then came Haycraft. Howard Haycraft produced in 1941 *Murder for Pleasure*, the best by far survey of what had been written up to that time.

It held sway, getting sadly slowly more and more out of date, until 1972 when Julian Symons wrote *Bloody Murder: From the Detective Story to the Crime Novel* and all was, as they say, light (even in America where the book was called *Mortal Consequences*). It has since gone into a second, updating, edition in 1985, and all is yet lighter.

Meanwhile in the stricter plain bibliographical area we had the pioneer listing of crime book after crime book in Ordean A. Hagen's *Who Done It?* of 1969, a somewhat erratic compilation to tell the truth. It has since been bettered decisively by Allen J. Hubin, first in 1979 with *The Bibliography of Crime Fiction*, then in 1984 with a revision *Crime Fiction 1749–1980*, massively marvellous. If you want to know whether any particular crime book exists, Hubin's your man. At a price.

In 1971 we got Jacques Barzun's and Wendell Hertig Taylor's *A Catalogue of Crime*, an assessment of no fewer than 7,500 books based on Professor Barzun's stern views of what detective fiction should be. Five years later came the first encyclopedia of crime writing called – what else? – *An Encyclopedia of Mystery and Detection*. It was edited by Chris Steinbrunner and Otto Penzler and is still unbeatable for the lives of crime writers, for accounts of their creations and for (beastly word) filmographies. But in some ways it was superseded by *Twentieth Century Crime and Mystery Writers*, edited by John M. Riley, in 1980 and revised in 1985, a fat and splendid tome replete with critical notices by various hands.

But for the ultimate in detail you should go to *Detective Fiction: the Collector's Guide*, published in 1988, and edited by John Cooper and B.A. Pike. It deals only with 105 of the most collected (by and large the most popular) crime authors, but about the outward shape of everything they have written in the mystery line it is, I think, unfaultable.

1 FEARFUL YELLOW

John D. MacDonald's Obsession

One fearful yellow what, you may well ask. The answer is, of course: *One Fearful Yellow Eye*, the title of John D. MacDonald's 1966 book about Travis McGee, who began as a baddie, more or less, specialising in recovering stolen goods, often from other criminals, and in recovering beautiful but mistreated girls by taking them for prolonged stays in his boat, won at poker, *The Busted Flush*, and who ended, pretty well, as a goody, an avenging private eye with a somewhat sloppy centre.

John D. MacDonald started him off, after writing a large number of paperback mysteries, in 1964 in a book he called *The Deep Blue Goodby* (in Britain *Goodbye*). Then, to establish another linking theme for the stories, he began to give each title a colour adjective, ending by using almost every shade in the paint charts. Here we go:

Pink, purple, red, gold, bright orange, amber, yellow, pale grey, plain brown, indigo, lavender, tan, scarlet, turquoise, dreadful lemon, copper, green (as in the green ripper = the Grim Reaper), crimson, cinnamon, silver. And what, as yet unmentioned, goes with them, not necessarily in the same order? Lonely rain, skin, free fall in, the empty sea, the sky, the lament, the ruse, a sandy silence, the long look, dress her in, the girl in the wrapper, for guilt, darker than, for the shroud, a deadly shade of, the quick fox, a place for dying, nightmare in.

Work it out.

SMELLING A RAT, OR A CLUE

Accused of not being a proper detective, the great Hercule Poirot in his second case *Murder On the Links* asks his much-teased Watson, Captain Hastings, if he ever goes fox-hunting. 'A bit,' Hastings replies. 'But,' says Poirot with that beastly triumphantness that has endeared him to the public ever since, 'you did not descend from your horse and run along the ground smelling with your nose?' Hastings takes the point. But, in later affairs, Poirot does indeed use his nose. Once, paralleling his famous predecessor's dog that did nothing in the night-time, he sniffs hard enough to detect an absence of tobacco smoke.

One at least of the recurring detectives, Horatio Green, the creation of the journalist and playwright Beverley Nichols (who wrote his autobiography at the age of twenty-five in 1926) depended for his successes largely on his nose. He was known to Scotland Yard, we are told, as the Human Bloodhound, thanks to the power of his 'olfactory sense'.

I'm afraid it must have been a memory of reading one of his cases that led me, only five years after Nichols abandoned the detective story in 1960 because reviewers were so hard on him, to give a one-off detective of mine, Superintendent Ironside, a similar readiness to use his nose. This was in *Is Skin-deep, Is Fatal*, a book about the beauty contest world (in which, villain that I am, I also pinched the central plot device from Agatha Christie's *The Murder of Rogert Ackroyd*). In it I had Ironside (not so much pinched from the American TV series as deliberately used since I felt the fellow could have no other name) step into the room where the murder had been committed and stand 'apparently gazing into space'. But he was detecting (shades of Sherlock: not another theft surely?) the absence of an odour, that of the electric fire there, which indicated to him that something else had been connected to the outlet not long before. A tape recorder? Clever man. Pity he was on the point of retirement.

AND THEN
THERE WERE NONE

The Christie Classic
Dismembered

Nice to come round full circle, like a classical detective story, and end a book that began by talking of Agatha Christie's title *Ten Little Niggers* by having a look at the book itself. We have started with the murdered body and are ending, as it were, with the murderer revealed.

Ten Little Niggers, as it was in Britain in 1940, is now on both sides of the Atlantic *And Then There Were None*, those dear innocent days when all good middle-class children in England had golliwog dolls and happily read *Little Black Sambo* having long passed away. But the Christie book remains, one of her best.

It stamps itself on the memory from the sheer intriguingness of its idea, and because of that Mrs Christie needed for it neither Hercule Poirot nor Miss Marple. To a small island off the south coast of England eight differing people are summoned to spend a mysterious holiday. Each of them, we learn in a series of admirably swift vignettes, has something in their past which casts a shadow.

When they reach the island their host appears not to be there, the only boat has been taken back by the boatman and there are only two servants, making a total of ten people stranded there. And the island, we learn, is called from its fancied resemblance to a negro's head – a not altogether persuasive point – Nigger Island. Soon, one by one the guests and the two servants start to be murdered.

The idea is stunning. Who will be next, you ask. And then, yet more intrigued, who will be the last left alive? Then, as the circle narrows, comes a yet more pertinent question: how will Agatha Christie get herself out of the situation she seems to have written herself into? How will she avoid the disappointment of any one of the few remaining alive proving to be the murderer? How will she fulfil the promise inherent in the last line of the rhyme she has dinned into us, 'and then there were none'? Indeed, she said in her autobiography that she wrote the book 'because it was difficult to do'.

The method she uses neatly to achieve that desirable end, while fairly unlikely both psychologically and mechanically, is that the actual final person left has to be relied on to commit suicide out of remorse for wrongdoing, and the real murderer has to kill himself using a complicated device with elastic masquerading as a ribbon on a pair of eyeglasses so as to deceive the police when they eventually arrive. Nevertheless it does adequately fulfil what might be called the fairy-story function of the book.

As with most of Agatha Christie's *tour-de-force* detective stories, *And Then There Were None* is, in fact, not an account of how a real crime might be perpetrated. Nor is it a novel, that is, a potentially credible simulacrum of real life. It is, instead, a juggling with the outward facts of life performed in order to create a satisfying puzzle. Books of this kind should be read for what they are, as by the average unliterary reader they generally are. It is only the more literary among us, working with a set of wrong expectations derived from the novel proper, who complain that stories of this type are too improbable. Ordinary readers are prepared to accept the improbabilities, just as, when children, they were prepared to accept the improbabilities of Hans Christian Andersen.

The point is underlined, unconsciously, by Agatha Christie herself in using a nursery rhyme to run through this book, as others have run through other books (*Five Little Pigs*, to use the British title, *Crooked House*, *A Pocket Full of Rye*, *Hickory, Dickory, Dock* and, another British title, *One, Two, Buckle My Shoe*). These are all excellent titles, not only for pointing to the fairy-tale element in the classical detective story, but also because of their innocence. Simultaneously they contrast the innocence of childhood with the evil of murder and assure a reader that the evil will be painted over in nursery colours.

So in *And Then There Were None* Agatha Christie not only arbitrarily changed the shape of Brownsea Island, her real-life model, as well as its name but she also placed in each bedroom in the house on the island a copy of the 'Ten Little Niggers' rhyme. Each of the murders, then, is to happen in accordance with the dictates of the

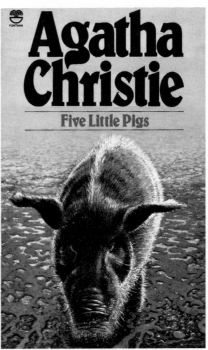

poem, another device that sanitises bloody death. This, to begin with, increases the tension as you, the reader, try to work out, for instance, just how the sixth victim is going to be killed after 'a bumble bee stung one and then there were five'. But the device does more than this: it gives the reader a strong feeling of Form.

Indeed, Form may be one of the reasons why Agatha Christie, with her strong feeling for it derived perhaps from her early serious study of music, was so successful a detective story writer. The detective story is a kind of fiction that more perhaps than any other obeys the dictates of form. It has its beginning with a murder (though it may have a pre-beginning with a murder about to be done); it has its widening expansion as the suspects one by one come into play, and perhaps come into play a second and a third time; it has its rapid drawing together as the detective nears his or her quarry; it comes to a final point, exactly echoing its beginning, when the murderer is named.

And to this necessary quality of Form Agatha Christie occasionally gave us a bonus in an underlining through a fairy cloak of nursery rhyme. In *And Then There Were None* she did this to perfection.

Numbers in italic refer to illustrations

A.B.C. Murders, The 14
Abbot, Anthony 41, 42
Above the Dark Circus 24
Act of Darkness 25
Adams, Samuel Hopkins 42
Adventure of the Speckled Band, The 62
Adventure of the Stalwart Companion,
    The 92
After the Funeral 14
Aird, Catherine 160
Album, The 172
Alexander, Lawrence 92
Allain, Marcel 49
Allingham, Margery 8, 42, 53, 68,
    176–8
Alphabet Murders, The 14
Ambler, Eric 58
And Then There Were None 13, 187–9
Anderson, Frederick Irving 51
Anything to Declare? 104
Appleby's End 80
Armstrong, Anthony 42
As If By Magic 65
Ask a Policeman 40
At Death's Door 68
Aubrey-Fletcher, Sir Henry Lancelot,
    40
Auden, W.H. 106, 108

Bailey, H.C. 64
Bait on the Hook 71
Ball, John 46
Barnard, Robert 68
Barr, Robert 71
Barrakee Mystery, The 32
Basil 143
Bat, The 170
Bawden, Nina 68
Beast Must Die, The 94, 94, 95
Behind the Screen 39
Behold, Here's Poison 102
Belloc Lowndes, Marie 89, 93, 121
Bennett, Arnold 24
Bentley, E.C. 20, 40, 75, 95, 96, 103
Bentley, Nicholas 75
Berkeley, Anthony 40–2
Bertie and the Tin Man 90
Beware of the Trains 80, 100
Big Bow Mystery, The 63
Big Fear, The 42
Big Sleep, The, 134, 135, 136
Big Stick, The 92
Birmingham, George 102
Black Beech and Honeydew 125
Black Tower, The 157, 158
Blackerchief Dick 176
Blackheath Poisonings, The 91
Blackmailers Don't Shoot 135
Blake, Nicholas 67, 94, 95
Blood Will Tell 14
Bloody Instructions 34
Bloody Murder or Mortal Consequences
    24, 36
Blue City 137, 137
Body in the Bush, The 38
Bogue's Fortune 64
Boomerang Clue, The 13
Boucher, Anthony 42, 83, 84
Boyd, Eunice May 42
Box, Edgar 24, 25
Brand, Christianna 42
Breen, John L. 75
Brett, Simon 100
Bride of Newgate, The 91, 91
Brides of Friedberg, The 20
Brighton Rock 8, 23
Brough, James C. 92
Bruce, Leo 74

Buried Alive 24
Burley, W.J. 69
Burton, Miles 36
Busted Flush, The 185
Butler, Gwendoline 19, 20, 93

Calamity Town 182
Canary Murder Case, The 63
Cargo of Eagles 19, 35, 178
Carr, John Dickson 19, 42, 61, 63, 64,
    72, 85, 89, 91, 173, 183
Case for Three Detectives 75
Case of the Marsden Rubies, The 43
Cat Among Pigeons 69
Cater Street Hangman, The 93
Chandler, Raymond 7, 37, 95,
    131–34, 149–53
Charteris, Leslie 44–46, 45, 59
Chesterton, G.K. 37, 39, 40, 49, 65, 82
Chinese Orange Mystery, The 63
Christie, Agatha 11, 13–17, 15, 36,
    39, 63, 68, 69, 73, 74, 77–9, 88,
    95–9, 118–22, 175, 176, 187–9
Circular Staircase, The 170, 172, 173
Clark, Douglas 69
Claverton Mystery, The 36
Clerical Error 20
Close Quarters 67, 132
Clouds of Witness 103
Clue of the New Pin, The 63
Coat of Arms, The 166
Coat of Varnish, A 24
Coffin for Pandora, A 19, 93
Coffin for the Canary, The 20
Cole, G.D.H and Margaret 36, 102
Colette 124
Collins, Wilkie 25, 50, 90, 91, 102,
    141–4
Conan Doyle, Sir Arthur 56, 62, 98,
    144–9
Cook, Stephen 70
Cooper, Henry St John 48
Cornish, George 42
Coroner's Pigeon 178
Corrector of Destinies, The 53
Craft of Crime, The 183
Creasey, John 48, 53
Creeping Man, The 94
Crime at Black Dudley, The 176
Crime at Diana's Pool, The 84
Crime on the Coast 43
Crispin, Edmund 65, 68, 80, 95, 99
Crocodile on the Sandbank 92
Crofts, Freeman Wills 36, 40, 42, 64,
    80, 81, 101, 104
Cronin, Michael 43
Crooked House 14
Cross, Amanda 67, 95, 129
Currington, O.J. 150
Curse of the Pharoahs, The 92
Curtain in the Rain 135

Dane, Clemence 40
Daniel, Glyn 129
Dannay, Fred 179–82, 181
Dark Tunnel, The 136
Daughter of Time, The 88, 90
Davidson, Lionel 119
Davies, Tony 132
Day Lewis, Cecil 67, 95
Dead Don't Scream, The 43
De Andrea, William 92
Dear Laura 93
Dear Miss Demeanor 67
Death at the Opera 68
Death at the President's Lodging 18, 19,
    129, 131
Death Before Bedtime 25
Death Cap 22
Death Comes at the End 88

Death in Captivity 132
Death in the Fifth Position 25
Death in the Stocks 20
Death is No Sportsman 104
Death Likes It Hot 25
Death of an Old Girl 70
Death of a Commuter 70
Death of a Millionaire 102
Death of a Peer 18
Death Prop 70
Death Under Sail 24
Deep Blue Goodby, The 185
de la Torre, Lillian 88
Denouement 110–11
Denver, Lee 43
Derleth, August 72
Destination Unknown 16
Detective Story 108
Detling Murders, The 91
Devil and Ben Franklin, The 92
Devine, D.M. 69
Dickens, Charles 25, 27, 88, 141
Dickinson, Peter 20, 21, 43
Dickson, Carter 64
Dirty Story 58
Dog It Was That Died, The 21
Don Among the Dead Men 20
Donnington Affair, The 39
Don't Guess Let Me Tell you 109
Doody, Margaret 88
Doomdorf Mystery, The 63
Double Death 42
Dr Sam Johnson: Detector 88, 90
Dumb Witness 14
Duncan, W. Murdoch 44
Durrant, Theo 42

Easy to Kill 14
Eberhart, M.G. 34
Eco, Umberto 86
Eliot, T.S. 141
Emily Dickinson is Dead 92
Eustace, Robert 61, 64
Eustis, Helen 66
Ewart, Gavin 116
Exploits of Sherlock Holmes, The 72

Fair, A.A. 44, 83
Faintley Speaking 68
Fairy Kist 25
Faulkner, Florence Ostern 42
Faulkner, William 23
Fear Comes to Chalfont 64
Fecamps, Elise 48
Fellowship of the Frog 166
Ferrars, Elizabeth 42, 83
Fighting Chance, A 34
Final Count, The 56
Final Problem, The 56
Fine, Anne 68
Fire, Burn! 91
Five Little Pigs 14, 188, 189
Five Red Herrings, The 38
Fleming, Joan 42
Floating Admiral, The 40
Ford, Leslie 102
Forester, C.S. 25
Four Just Men, The 166, 167
Freeman, R. Austin 104, 160–2
Fremlin, Celia 11
Friday the Rabbi Slept Late 87, 87
Frome, David 102
Frye, Northrop 95
Funerals Are Fatal 14
Futrelle, Jacques 168, 169

Gaines, Donald 150
Galton Case, The 136, 138, 139
Gardner, Erle Stanley 44, 46, 53, 145

Gardner, John 73
Gash, Jonathan 52
Gilbert, Anthony 42
Gilbert, Michael 67, 132
Gill, B.M. 70
Glass-sided Ants' Nest, The 20, 21, *22*
Glimpses of the Moon, The 99
Godey, John 76
Go West, Inspector Ghote 65
Golden Rain 69
Goodby 185
Gores, Joe 119
Grand Babylon Hotel, The 24
Grant, Landon 44
Greene, Graham 8, 23, 77, 78
Grella, Professor George 173
Grex, Leo 43
Gribble, Leonard 43
Grimes, Martha 29, 30, *32*
Guilty Party, The 112–13

Hair of the Sleuthhound 75
Hamlet, Revenge! 130
Hammett, Dashiel 51, 150, *152*
Hannay, Canon J.O. 102
Hansford Johnson, Pamela 24, 177
Hare, Cyril 104, 132
Hartley, L.P. 8
He Didn't Kill Patience 65
Heilbrun, Professor Carolyn 83, 129
Hell of a Writer, A 117
Henisart, Martha 183
Her Death of Cold 86
Hercule Poirot's Christmas 14
Hess, Joan 67
Heyer, Georgette 20, 102
Hickory, Dickory Death 16
Hickory, Dickory Dock 16, 188
Highsmith, Patricia 18, 30, 43, 58, 70, 77, 153–6
Hilda Wade: A Woman of Great Tenacity of Purpose 35
Hill, Reginald 110–11
Hilton, James 67
Himes, Chester 150
His Own Appointed Day 69
Hoch, Ed 60
Holiday for Murder, A 14
Holmes, H.H. 84, 89
Hollow Man, The 19, 64, 85
Hollow, The 14
Holton, Leonard 85, 86
Horizontal Man, The 66
Hound of the Baskervilles, The 144–9, *149*
Hornung, E.W. 57, 58, 73
House of Cain, The 32
H.R.H. the Prince of Wales: An Account of his Career 121
Hughes, Dorothy B. 170
Human Factor, The 23
Hume, David 42
Hungry Goblin, The 91
Hymson, Allen 42

Iles, Francis 40
In the Heat of the Night 46
In the Last Analysis 83
Innes, Michael 17, 80, 95, 96, 128–31
Inspector Ghote Draws a Line 29
Inspector Ghote Goes By Train 80, *81*

James, Breni 88
James, P.D. 156–9, *158*
Jeffers, H. Paul 92
Jenkins, Cecil 129
Jepson, Edgar 40, 61
Jepson, Selwyn 40, 64
Jesse, F. Tennyson 42

Kemelman, Harry 87
Kennedy, Milward 39–41

Kidnapped Baby Blake, Millionaire 169
Kienzle, William 88
Killer in the Rain 135
Killjoy, The 68
King, Francis 25
Kipling, Rudyard 40, 42
Knox, Ronald 40, 42

Lady Vanishes, The 79, *79*
Lament for a Maker 130, *130*
Lament for Leto 174
Langton, Jane 18, 92
Late, Late in the Evening 174
Lathan, Emma 49, 183
Latsis, Jane 183
Laurels are Poison 105
Leblanc, Maurice 53, 54
Le Carré, John 69
Lee, Manfred 179–82, *181*
Lemarchand, Elizabeth 69, 70
Leroux, Gaston 63, 122
Light of Day, The 58
Little House at Croix-Rouge, The 65
Locked Room, The 65
Lodger, The 93, 121
Long Journey Home, The 132
Loot of Cities, The 24
Lorac, E.C.R 42
Lord Edgware Dies 13
Love Lies Bleeding 68
Lovesey, Peter 46, 90
Lucas, Cary 42
Lunatic Fringe, The 92
Lyon, Dana 42

MacDonald, John D. 185
MacDonald, Ross 136–9, *137*
MacKenzie, Donald 150
MacLeod, Charlotte 96
McDonald, Gregory 119
McInerney, Ralph 86, 87
Mainwaring, Marion 75
Maltese Falcon, The 51, 149–53
Man in Lower Ten, The 170
Man Lay Dead, A 126
Man Overboard 104
Man Who Lost His Wife, The 95
Man Who Wrote Detective Stories, The 131
Marble Forest, The 42
Marric, J.J. 48
Marsh, Ngaio 18, 19, 125–8, *127*
Masterman, Sir John 129
Mary Postgate 25
Mathieson, Theodore 92
Maugham, Somerset 149
Meadowsweet 20
Meet the Baron 53
Merely Murder 20
Message from Sirius 129
Meyer, Nicholas 72
Meynell, Laurence 42, 43
Midnight Specials 76
Millar, Kenneth 136–9
Milne, A.A. 96
Mind Readers, The 178
Ministry of Fear, The 23
Minuteman Murder, The 92
Mirror Crack'd from Side to Side, The 17
Mitchell, Gladys 18, 41, 42, 68, 95, 105, 173–5
Moonstone, The 25, 90, 102, 140–4, *140, 142*
Morbid Taste for Bones, A 86
More Work for the Undertaker 178
Moriarty Journals, The 73
Morton, Anthony 53
Mouse That Roared, The 85
Moving Target, The 137
Moving Toyshop, The 99, *100*

Mr Pottermack's Overnight 104, *161*, *162*
Mrs McGinty's Dead 14
Muir, Dexter 43
Murder After Hours 14
Murder at Hazelmoor, The 13
Murder at School 67
Murder At the Gallop 14
Murder for Christmas 14
Murder in Pastiche 75
Murder in Retrospect 14
Murder in the Calais Coach 13, 76
Murder in Three Acts 13
Murder is Easy 14
Murder of Quality, A 69
Murder on the Blackboard 66
Murder on the Orient Express 13, 76, 77
Murder on the Sixth Hole 102
Murder She Said 16
Murder with Mirrors 14
Murder's A Swine 24
Murders in the Rue Morgue, The 6, 7, 61, 62
My Bones Will Keep 174
Mysterious Affair at Styles, The 118, 120, *120*, 176
Mystery Mile 176
Mystery of Angelina Frood, The 160
Mystery of Edwin Drood, The 25, 26
Mystery of Mr Jessop, 37
Mystery of the Blue Train, The 78, *78*
Mystery of the Yellow Chamber, The 63, *63*
Mystery of the Yellow Room, The 122

Naked Villainy 34
Name of the Rose, The 86
Narcejac, Thomas 125
Nash, Ogden 109
Newby, Eric, 132
Night of Secrets 42
Night of the Twelfth, The 67
Night of Wenceslas, The 119
Nine Tailors, The 9, 9, 30, 31
Nine Times Nine 85
Nobody's Perfect 99
Not One of Us 22
No Flowers By Request 42

Oaken Heart, The 178
Odd Flamingo, The 68
Offord, Leonore Glen 42
Oh! Where are Bloody Mary's Earrings? 92
Old English Peep Show, The 21
Old Fox Deceiv'd, The 29
Olivia 20
One Fearful Yellow Eye 185
One, Two, Buckle My Shoe 14, 188, *189*
Oursler, Fulton 41
Overdose of Death, An 14
Owl Who Wrote a Detective Story, The 116
Oxford Tragedy, An 129

Paddington Mystery, The 36
Palmer, Stuart 66, 98
Papa La Bas 91
Paper Chase, The 68
Parody Party 75
Parrish, Frank 71
Partners in Crime 73, 97
Passenger From Scotland Yard, The 79, 80
Patriotic Murders, The 14
Paul, Raymond 91
Payment Deferred 25
Pearce, Michael 92
Pemberton, Sir Max 37
Perowne, Barry 73
Perry, Anne 93
Peters, Elizabeth 92

Peters, Ellis 86, 88
Peters, Stephen 92
Pin to See the Peepshow, A 42
Plain Murder 25
Player on the Other Side 180, 182
Player, Robert 92
Pocket Full of Rye, A 14, 98, 99, 188
Poe, Edgar Allan 7, 30, 84, 88, 145, 169
Poetic Justice 67
Poirot Loses a Client 14
Police at the Funeral 177
Post, Melville Davisson 53, 63, 84, 163–5
Postern of Fate 97
President's Mystery Story, The 42
Pride of Heroes, A 21
Priestley, J.B. 24
Problem of Cell 13, The 168, 169, *169*
Pronzini, Bill 76
Punshon, E.R. 36, 37, 105

Queen, Ellery 63, 66, 88, 89, 179–82
Question of Proof, A 67
Quill, Monica 87

Rampe, Edogawa 83
Rath, Virginia 42
Rawson, Clayton 65
Red House Mystery, The 96
Red Thumb-mark, The 162
Remembered Death 14
Rhode, John 36, 40
Rice, Craig 98
Riley, Tex 48
Rinehart, Mary Roberts 170–3, *171*
Ripley's Game 155
Ripley Under Ground 155
Rising of the Moon, The 175
Rocket to the Morgue 85
Rohmer, Sax 54
Rolls, Anthony 20
Roman Hat Mystery, The 179
Roosevelt, Franklin 41
Rosary Murders, The 88
Ross, Barnaby 182
Routley, Dr Erik 10, 82
Rush on the Ultimate, A 69

Safer Than Love 68
Saint Maker, The 85
Salt is Leaving 24
Sands of Windee, The 32–34, *33*
Sarsen Place 20
Sartre, Jean-Paul 54
Sayers, Dorothy L. 9, 18, 30, 31, 39–42, 65, 97, 98, 103
Scandal at High Chimneys, The 91
Scandal of Father Brown, The 82
Schoolmaster, The 69
Scoop, The 40
Seals, The 22
Secret Adversary, The 96, 97
Secret of Father Brown, The 82, 82, 84
Send for Lord Timothy 114–15
Seven per Cent Solution, The 72
Seven Suspects 18, 129
Shattuck, Richard 42
Sheiks and Adders 95
Simenon, Georges 46, 47, 65, 123–5
Simpson, Helen 40, 41
Sinful Stones, The 22
Sir John Magill's Last Journey 81, 101
Sittaford Mystery, The 13
Situation Tragedy 100
Six Against the Yard 42
Six Suspects 38
Six Unlikely Persons 38
Sjöwall, Maj 65, *65*
Skin Deep 21
Sleepers of Erin, The 52
Sleeping Murder 17

Smartest Grave, The 93, 129
Snow, C.P. 23, 24
So Many Steps to Death 16
Souvestre, Pierre 49
Sparkling Cyanide 14
Speedy Death 174
Stamboul Train 77
Stewart, Gordon 24
Stewart, J.I.M. 129–31
Stout, Rex 46, 46, 47, 173
Street, Major Cecil 36
Strangers on a Train 76
Stubbs, Jean 93
Stubbs, John Heath 114–15
Study in Scarlet, A 11
Surfeit of Lampreys 18
Sweet Adelaide 91
Swimming Pool, The 172
Symons, Julian 24, 36, 43, 65, 68, 91, 92, 95, 112–13

Taken at the Flood 14
Taking of Pelham 123, The 76
Talented Mr Ripley, The 153–9
Taste for Death, A 156–9
Taste for Power, A 69
Tea-Leaf, The 61
Teilhet, Darwin 42
Tell-tale Heart, The 88
Ten Little Indians 13
Ten Little Niggers 13, 187–9
Tey, Josephine 88
Theban Mysteries, The 95
There is a Tide . . . 16
There's One Thing Missing 38
They Do It With Mirrors 16
Third Man, The 23
This Gun for Hire 23
Thirteen at Dinner 13
Thomas Street Horror, The 91
Thomson, June 22
Thorndike, Russell 42
Three-Act Tragedy 14
Three Coffins, The 19, *19*, 64, 85
Three Oaks Mystery, The 166
Three Roads, The 137
Thrilling Stories of the Railway 40
Thursday the Rabbi Walked Out 87
Tidy Death 24
Tiger in the Smoke, The 8, *177*, 178
Tom Brown's Body 68
Tragedy at Tiverton 91
Transcendental Murder, The 92
Tremor of Forgery, A 154
Trent's Last Case 20, *21*, 40, 96, 103
Trevor, Glen 67
Triumphs of Eugene Valmont, The 71
Trouble Follows Me 136
Trout in Milk, A 64
Twain, Mark 71

Uncle Abner, Master of Mysteries 85, 163
Underwood, Michael 43, 64, 70
Unnatural Death 31
Upfield, Arthur 31–34
Upperdown 70

Valley of Fear, The 56
Van Dine, S.S 42, 63, 83, 182
Vance, Louis Joseph 52
Verdict of Thirteen 43
Vicar's Experiments, The 20
Victim of Circumstances 70
Vidal, Gore 24
Vulliamy, C.E. 20

Wade, Henry 40
Wahlöö, Per 65, *65*
Wall, The 172
Wallace, Edgar 44, 63, 165–7, *167*
Walpole, Hugh 24, 39

Warriner, Thurman 85
Watson, Colin 59
Wentworth Patricia 175
Westlake, Donald E. 99
What Mrs McGillycuddy Saw 16, 79
Wheel Spins, The 79
When Last I Died 174
White, Ethel Lina 79
White, R.J. 93, 129
White, Valerie 43
Whitechurch, Canon Victor 40, 84
Whose Body? 97, *98*
Why Didn't They Ask Evans 13
Why Shoot the Butler? 102
Wild Justice 102
Williams, Valentine 42
Wilson, Edmund 8–10
Witch at Low Tide, The 91
Woddis, Roger 117
Woman in Black, The 20, *103*
Woman in White, The 50, *50*
Woman Who Did, The 35
Wood, H.E. 79, 80
Woodcock, George 23
Woods, Sara 34
Worley, William 42
Wright, Huntingdon Willard 182

Zangwill, Israel 63, *63*

4.50 from Paddington 16, *17*, 79
813 53

ILLUSTRATION SOURCES

Aitken & Stone Ltd: 15

The Hulton Picture Library (The Bettmann Archive Inc.): 105

The Kobal Collection: 79

Photograph by Robin Lubbock: 32

Otto Penzler: 9, 16, 19 (2), 31, 41, 45 below left, 46 (2), 50, 51, 57 right, 62, 65 right, 77, 78, 81, 82 (2), 85, 87, 90 (2), 91, 98 right, 100 left, 101, 121, 124 (2), 127, 134, 137 right, 140, 142, 146, 152 left, 155, 158 (2), 167 top, 177

Edgar Allan Poe *The Murders in the Rue Morgue* (George Harrap, London, 1919) illustrations by Harry Clark: 6

Lord Peter Wimsey illustrated by John Campbell from 'The Dragon's Head' for *Pearson's*, 1926: 10